BUFFALO
BRENDA
JILL PINKWATER

MACMILLAN PUBLISHING COMPANY   NEW YORK

Macmillan Publishing Company, 866 Third Avenue, New York, NY 10022.
Collier Macmillan Canada, Inc.
First Edition   Printed in the United States of America

10 9 8 7 6 5 4 3 2 1

The text of this book is set in 11 point Goudy Old Style.

Library of Congress Cataloging-in-Publication Data
Pinkwater, Jill. Buffalo Brenda / by Jill Pinkwater.—1st ed.   p.   cm.
Summary: Determined to make their mark on their high school, ninth graders
India Ink and her zany best friend Brenda Tuna organize an underground
newspaper and then provide a live buffalo as a mascot for the football team.
ISBN 0–02–774631–3
[1. Journalism—Fiction.   2. Bison—Fiction.   3. High Schools—Fiction.
4. Schools—Fiction.]   I. Title.
PZ7.P6336Bu   1989   [Fic]—dc19   88–31929   CIP   AC

For my friend

CAITLIN

with love

∇ ∇ ∇

ONE

IT was Sunday morning. I had exactly twenty-four hours left on earth before facing my doom. I was about to become a freshman at Florence Senior High School. Where was Brenda when I needed her the most? Off having fun with her family—too busy to write letters for most of the summer. Why wasn't she back yet?

I stared into the bathroom mirror, realizing that I had wasted money on the superstrength, cover-and-cure, invisible blemish cream. I rubbed another glob onto my chin. It became invisible, all right—instantly. My "blemish" shone through like a Christmas light.

"I'd demand my money back." Brenda's unique, foggy voice made me jump.

"Can't. I ordered it through the mail." I tried to be cool, but I failed. I whirled around and screamed, "You're back! Finally!" I hugged my friend, who was standing in the bathroom doorway. Her dark tan almost covered what looked like at least a couple of hundred insect bites.

"Did you really think I'd let a little thing like a family trip up the Amazon make me miss the very beginning of our glorious high-school years? Besides, my father stepped on a poisonous snake a couple of weeks ago—not to worry—he lived. After he recovered, he kind of lost his enthusiasm for tropical places."

"You grew." I stared at my friend, who was now at least two inches taller than I.

"It happens," said Brenda.

"Don't you itch, Brenda? I never saw so many bug bites on one person in my life."

1

"When you're in the Amazon jungle, after meeting up with hostile Indians, piranhas, and snakes, you're grateful that the bugs are the only things biting you. Which reminds me, I'm starved. Let's eat breakfast and make plans. We shall sweep into that school tomorrow and conquer it with our style and wit. We'll be the outstanding stars in high school that we should have been in junior high."

"Brenda, we're freshmen. We're starting all over again. Square one. We're going to be nobodies. Nonentities. We're so low in the order of things that we don't even know where the girls' rooms are."

"They'll be labeled," said Brenda. "Let's go to the diner. Breakfast is on me. I didn't get a chance to spend a penny of my allowance all summer."

"No pizza places in the jungle?"

"Not any you'd care to visit," said Brenda.

"I can't imagine not having you as a friend," I said.

"Do you remember the day we first met?"

"I also remember what my family thought of you."

▽ ▽ ▽

"THERE'S no accounting for taste!" mumbled Smoke through a mouthful of food.

"Swallow before you speak," said my mother.

"Weird," continued Smoke.

"*Smoke*," warned my mother.

"It's disgusting sitting next to you at dinner, Pig Slop," said Rain, moving her chair as far from Smoke as she could. "Besides, who are you to call anyone else weird?"

"Living in this house with *you* gives me the right." Smoke smiled, purposely oozing chewed food from between his teeth.

2

"Mother, stop him," pleaded Rain. "I'm going to throw up all over the table."

"If you do that, you'll never eat another meal in this house." My father was looking at Rain and Smoke as if two Martians had suddenly landed in our kitchen. "Why can't we ever have an interesting conversation at our dinner table instead of the usual drivel—and why must you pick at each other? And while we're on the subject, how come you're so silent, India? You're usually right in the middle of the Teidlebaum Family Demolition Derby."

My mother giggled. She thought my father was the funniest man in the world. "India's probably being quiet because it's her new friend they're discussing, Steven."

"India met someone strange at school?"

"I wouldn't exactly call her strange. Let's just say she's a little peculiar."

"How so?" asked my father.

"Why don't you start with her name?" Smoke guffawed, spewing particles of food all over the table.

"That is disgusting, son. Your sister was right about your table manners. If you speak, laugh, spit, or even breathe with your mouth open before swallowing your food one more time . . . note the number involved now . . . *one* . . . got it?" My father paused and waited for Smoke to nod his head. "I am going to think of a punishment so horrible, you will be sorry you were ever born." My father smiled. Smoke didn't dare do anything until he swallowed. Rain looked pleased.

"Harsh," muttered Smoke.

"Isn't that a bit extreme, Steven?" Although my mother enjoys my father's sense of humor, she often can't tell if he is being serious. To be honest, neither can the rest of us. It gives my father a great advantage in moments of conflict.

3

"Maybe, but the problem is solved, isn't it, Smoke?"

Smoke took a big swallow of milk to make sure all food was washed out of his mouth and answered politely, "Yes, Dad."

"Good. Now what's this about India's new friend?"

"First of all, her name is Tunafish. Brenda Tunafish." Smoke dissolved into a fit of laughing.

"Tunafish?" My father was smiling. "Brenda Tunafish? Must have found her in the fish store." Now my mother was laughing.

"Okay. That's it. Enough. This family has some nerve. First of all, her name is Brenda Tuna. T-U-N-A, not tuna fish. Secondly, in a home where the mother and father voluntarily named their innocent children Smoke, Rain, and India Ink Teidlebaum, there is very little room for making fun of the names of others." I stood up on my chair to get the full attention of the family. It was a technique I had learned from Brenda just that week.

"India, get off that chair." My mother has always been afraid that we would fall off or out of things. We are forbidden to climb ladders, step stools, trees, and mountains until we are twenty-one.

"Teidlebaum was your father's last name when I married him," my mother mused. "We didn't choose it to give you, it was just there." She winked at my father.

"Not *Teidlebaum*, Mother. You voluntarily named us Smoke, Rain, and India Ink."

"Rain came first. She was born during such a gentle spring shower. The whole mountainside smelled of fresh growing grass." My mother was smiling at my father.

"Rain isn't a normal kid name, Mother! Neither is Smoke. And India Ink is positively bizarre!" I had previously tried to make this point with no success. Before my mother could launch into her story about how she was sketching the essence of the night sky by firelight when she went into labor with me, I tried to get back to the original subject.

I sat down and spoke to my father. "Brenda is my best friend."

"So soon? You've been in junior high for less than two weeks. Friendship takes time to cultivate—to grow."

"I've been in junior high for fifteen days, which is more than two weeks, but . . ."

"You're counting the weekends," Smoke interrupted. I ignored him and continued.

"Brenda says time doesn't matter. In life, real bonds happen instantly. She calls it natural affinity and says it can work with most important things in life, such as puppies and kittens and horses and art and relationships."

"I told you, Steven, peculiar." My mother was shaking her head.

"I don't know, Carol. This Brenda kid seems to have an interesting point of view. However, I don't like the idea of India hanging around with older kids."

"Older? Brenda is my age. She's in my homeroom."

"Then Brenda is pretty smart for a seventh grader." My father looked impressed.

"I'm not sure, Steven. You have to meet the child to evaluate her. She doesn't seem"—my mother searched for the right word and came up with—"normal."

I got really angry. "Hey. *Hey!* Do as I say and not as I do, right, Mom? Where were you living when Rain was born—in a tent, right? Was that normal for a college graduate from New York City? And who delivered her? I've heard the stories. It was your good buddy Crystal Chrysanthemum, the Vassar dropout who grew up in Connecticut as Janet Headly-Smith. Was that

5

normal? In fact, was *she* normal?

"And how about me? By the time I arrived, you were living in a teepee in a state park. You named *me* after the ink you were using to draw your dumb pictures of the cosmos. Was *that* normal?" I stared at my mother, who looked puzzled.

"I wish you'd understand, India, dear. Your name is so poetic. It's so meaningful. Those were special times. Your father and I went to the wilderness to find our centers. You three were part of that."

"Fine, so now your centers are the brokerage firm and the country club and the stupid mall, and we're stuck with three creepy names, you phonies!" I suspected that I had gone a little too far.

"You, too, can suffer a horrible, devastating punishment, India." My father did not look as if he were making one of his jokes.

"Superharsh," said Smoke. "Aren't you going to talk about how I was born on the commune?"

"Butt out, Disgusto," said Rain. "Give the kid sister room to maneuver."

"Do you really think I am a phony?" asked my mother quietly. She looked ready to cry.

"I'm sorry I said that, Mom. But you have become the most superstraight person I know—and that includes Dad."

"Me, superstraight?" asked my mother.

"Your mother, superstraight?" asked my father. He turned and studied my mother.

"Both of you," I answered.

"Both of us?" They stared at each other, shaking their heads.

"It's not just the way you dress and live, it's your minds. You don't leave room for ideas anymore."

6

"How awful," said my mother.

"That isn't true," said my father.

"So why are you judging Brenda? You haven't even met her yet, Dad. Brenda says prejudgment is the foundation of bigotry."

"Brenda said that?" asked my father. "How old did you say she is?"

"Same as me. Actually, she's about a year younger because they skipped her one grade. She's eleven and a half."

"And she's talking about affinity and bigotry and relationships?" My father was having a hard time accepting the idea of Brenda.

"She's very unusual," I said. "She thinks a lot."

"That's a better adjective," added my mother. "Let's delete the word *peculiar* from the description of Brenda."

"Thanks, Mom. I know you'll get to like Brenda once you get to know her."

My mother smiled but didn't look too confident.

"Delete *peculiar*, add *unusual*, and insert PHILOSOPHER!" Smoke shouted. Then he made noises like a spinning disk-drive on a computer.

"Philosopher," said my mother. "That's good, Smoke."

"The Philosopher," said my father.

"The Kid Philosopher," added Rain.

"Her name is Brenda," I yelled, but it was too late.

▽ ▽ ▽

IN the two years since that conversation took place, no member of my family has ever used Brenda Tuna's real name. She became and remains, "The Philosopher," "The Kid Philosopher," and, to her face, just plain "Philosopher."

7

Brenda says she likes the title. She says it's got both status and class.

▽ ▽ ▽

TWO

"AREN'T you in the least bit nervous about tomorrow?" I asked Brenda.

"No, why should I be? No matter what happens, it can't possibly be worse than walking into junior high for the first time," said Brenda, munching on the pizza that was our fourth meal of the day.

"Come off it, Bren. There was never a more confident kid in the entire history of Florence Junior High."

"Not so. Appearances are often deceiving, India. My strange and eccentric behavior during those early days was simply a way of covering up the fact that I felt I was too young, too short, and too round for junior high." Brenda looked philosophical.

"*You* were afraid? You've never, *ever* admitted that before." I was shocked.

"I didn't realize it before. I was terrified of being among all those large adolescents. The circumstances of this Amazonian family vacation—which was almost our last vacation as a family—forced me to think about my entire life."

"If you didn't know you were afraid, then you can't say you were afraid," I insisted.

"Yes, I can," said Brenda.

"Phooey," I said.

"You've lost some of your eloquence over the summer, haven't you?" said Brenda.

"Sometimes I think I'd like to wrap a rubber chicken around your neck," I grumbled.

"See what I mean?" Brenda wiped her mouth, brushed pizza crumbs from her shirt, and said, "I really missed you, India. Do you remember how we met?"

"How could I ever forget?"

▽ ▽ ▽

MY first day of junior high had a predictably grim start. I missed the bus. When I got to school, I wandered the halls with several hundred other confused seventh graders—all nervously clutching semisquashed registration papers in their hands—until I found room 212. I started to smile as I crossed into the first homeroom of my school career. I stopped smiling almost immediately.

A tall, bony, sour-looking man was sitting at the teacher's desk, scowling into a book and ignoring the arriving students. Behind him, the chalkboard was covered with large, clear writing. It said:

INFORMATION FOR HOMEROOM

1. Mister Osgood, Teacher of English, Creative Writing, and, unfortunately, Homeroom
2. THERE IS NO DEMOCRACY WITHIN THIS CLASSROOM.
3. Find a seat, place yourself in it, and do not talk.
4. THESE ARE ORDERS, NOT REQUESTS.
5. Put your registration forms on your desk.
6. Have a pencil ready to use.
7. Wait, and memorize the following:

NONNEGOTIABLE HOMEROOM RULES

IN THIS CLASSROOM THERE WILL BE NO

WHISPERING, PENCIL CHEWING, EARPHONE WEARING, SPITTING, NOTE PASSING, BACK TALKING, UNAUTHORIZED TALKING OF ANY KIND, NAIL BITING, HAT WEARING, RADIO CARRYING, LAUGHING, GIGGLING, SNICK-ERING, TEETH SUCKING.

DISREGARDING ANY OF THESE RULES WILL LEAD TO INSTANT AND HORRIBLE RETRI-BUTION. I HAVE NO MERCY.

The seats toward the back of the room and next to the windows had all been taken, the early arrivals having moved as far away from Mr. Osgood as possible. To avoid having to walk in front of a room half full of strangers, I just slid behind the first empty desk I saw. It happened to be in the front row next to the door. Quick escape! is the thought that entered my mind.

Kids kept straggling in long after the bell had rung. By ten after eight, the room was pretty full. Mr. Osgood, Teacher of English, stood up. He had looked tall sitting down, but standing up he was impressive. All of us in the first three rows had to tilt our heads back to see his face.

"One of you is missing," boomed Mr. Osgood. He must have been keeping count as we arrived. "*You,*" he said, pointing to me, "close the door."

I instantly remembered the disadvantage of sitting near a classroom door. I got up and shut it as quietly as possible. Just as I sat down, the door flew open with such force that it slammed against the rubber stopper on the wall and bounced closed again. A hand stopped it from shutting completely. Then slowly, the door opened again, and the most exotic kid I had ever seen sauntered into the room. She was so odd-looking that, despite the fear generated by Mr. Osgood standing facing them, most of the kids started to giggle.

The girl walked up to Mr. Osgood, smiled, and put out her hand to shake his. Naturally he refused to return the courtesy. She shrugged her shoulders, glanced at the chalkboard, and read it before coolly walking to the remaining empty seat in the room—which just happened to be directly in front of where Mr. Osgood was standing. Then she did something that stopped the giggling and held the attention of the entire class for about sixty seconds. Never pausing, never seeming to stall, always in motion, the girl took a whole minute to sit down.

If Mr. Osgood hadn't turned red in the face, I think the class would have applauded. Comfortably settled in her place, the girl beamed up at Mr. Osgood, who grabbed his black roll book. "Answer *present* when I say your name," he growled, and began calling the roll.

This was the part I most dreaded. With the exception of Suzie Stein, who had been the cutest, most stuck-up kid in my old elementary school, and Steve Kelly, the biggest jerk from my former sixth-grade class, I didn't know a single kid in my homeroom. Mr. Osgood quickly worked his way up to the *p*'s. There were no *q*'s, only three *r*'s, and two *s*'s. I braced myself.

"Teidlebaum, India Ink? Is this some kind of joke?" The class started to titter. I could hear Suzie's nauseating giggle leading the pack.

"No, sir. It's my actual name. Please call me India." My voice squeaked as I spoke. I could feel my face getting hot. Now Steve was snorting, which seemed to encourage the other boys to make equally horrible noises.

"Answer *present* when I call your name. No back talk is

necessary." Mr. Osgood turned his attention to the class. "QUIET!" he shouted, and pointed to the last line written on the chalkboard. I thought my eardrums would break. Everyone froze in midlaugh. I took the opportunity to speak.

"I wasn't talking back, Mr. Osgood. I thought you had asked me a question." Sometimes I do not know when to keep my mouth shut.

"*That* is back talk. No one speaks in this room unless he or she has something of import to say. For those of you who are illiterate dolts, *import* means something important. Important, in this classroom, can be defined as important to *me*. Do you understand, class?"

Some kids started to say yes, but Mr. Osgood gave them a nasty look. "Nod your heads. Do not use your vocal chords! I shall continue—without interruption. Tuna, Brenda. Another bizarre name to provoke idiotic laughter." Mr. Osgood scowled. The class had begun giggling again. It stopped abruptly when the students noticed the look on Mr. Osgood's mean face.

"Is there any mistake in the spelling of your name, young lady—T-U-N-A—like the fish?"

"Present," answered the exotic girl in the front row.

"I asked you a question, Miss Tuna."

"You explicitly told us not to say anything but *present*. I am trying to conform to your orders. Present," said Brenda Tuna again.

"That's enough sass, young lady. Answer my question, or, like the fish you are named after, I shall make sure you are caught, processed, and canned in the detention room for the rest of the year." The classroom was suddenly very quiet.

"I would rather be named Tuna than shark, sir," answered Brenda. She was still smiling sweetly at Mr. Osgood. As she spoke, she kind of slid down in her chair and draped one arm over its back. This allowed her to look up at the tall fiend without straining her neck.

I noticed that all the kids in the first three rows followed her example. Before Mr. Osgood could make good on his threat, Brenda added, "And, yes, my name is Tuna—T-U-N-A."

Mr. Osgood glared at Brenda Tuna. "Do you always dress in that outlandish fashion, Miss Tuna?"

"I don't know what you are talking about, Mr. Osgood. Are you referring to the national costume of my native country?" Brenda gestured toward her extremely colorful outfit.

"You are not a native of the United States?" asked Mr. Osgood.

"I am a citizen of the world, and my attire reflects that citizenship."

Never had a truer word been spoken. Brenda Tuna's skirt, blouse, shoes, headband, and jewelry looked like they had been snatched from random pages of *National Geographic*. Even her dark, curly hair was partly braided with beads and ribbons. Nothing on her matched, but all together, her articles of clothing did make an outfit—a bright, pretty, and very strange outfit.

"There is a dress code in this school, young lady."

"I do not think I am breaking it, sir," said Brenda Tuna politely.

The whole class knew Brenda was right. The code forbid kids to wear things like tight leather pants, shorts, miniskirts, or, in general, any item of clothing that revealed "too much" of one's body. There was absolutely nothing in the code about articles of clothing from different parts of the world. Mr. Osgood knew he was defeated. He looked at his watch and walked back to his desk. From there he called the rest of the roll and took care of first-day business.

We handed in our registration forms, filled in duplicates of our programs, and were generally read the riot act. Along with his attitude about free speech, Mr. Osgood did not approve of tardiness, rowdiness, or, it seemed, much of anything. He also did not approve of changing seats. Where you sat that first day was where you would sit for the entire year. When the bell finally rang, twenty-eight depressed seventh graders quietly filed into the hallway and shuffled off to find their first-period classes.

"He's a real trip, isn't he?" someone said cheerfully.

"A trip? Osgood? He's like having Attila the Hun for homeroom," I answered. Brenda Tuna was walking next to me.

"No, not Attila, really. *He* was a barbarian. Mr. Osgood, Teacher of English, considers himself a civilized man."

"You speak like an adult," I said.

"Does it bother you?" Brenda asked.

"No, why should it?"

"Because I've spoken this way for years and years and it's always bothered my peers."

"Your peers?"

"People who are about my age and who supposedly are my equals."

"I know what peers are. What do you mean by *supposedly?*" I wondered if Brenda thought the rest of us were inferior to her.

"No two people are exactly alike. Each person has interests, abilities, strong and weak points. Some are dull and some are interesting. Some are gifted and some are ordinary. Some are bright and some are stupid. Some are beautiful and some are plain. How can you say people are equal—are peers—just because they share a year of birth?

"Equal under the law—certainly. Equal in God's eyes—certainly. Deserving equal treatment and courtesy and respect—certainly. But I believe that in the end we are all peerless."

"You're blocking the stairs, Brenda," I said.

Brenda had stopped in the narrow stairwell to explain her theory of peers to me and the twenty or so other students temporarily trapped there. She did not move an inch until she had finished her speech. Neither did the rest of us.

"These acoustics are great," she said loudly when I finally managed to pull her to the landing so the kids could pass. Her voice echoed off the walls.

"What's your next class?" I asked.

"Science."

"Me, too. What room?"

"Three thirty-seven."

"Me, too." We compared schedules. Brenda and I had most of the same classes. One of them was English with Mr. Osgood.

"At least we'll be together, India Ink." Brenda winked at me.

"Right, Tuna." I winked back.

▽ ▽ ▽

THREE

DURING lunch that day, Brenda and I exchanged stories about how we got our names. I told Brenda about my mother's mystical experience with the cosmos. Brenda told me about her grandfather, Vladimir Tunitsky.

Vladimir emigrated to the United States from Eastern Europe. Six months after his arrival, he married Miru, whom he had met at the Rumanian Social Club. One year after that, Vladimir and Miru, having learned much English and many American customs, felt that they would blend in faster and better if they Americanized their names. They consulted with their

15

friends—who happened to be mostly other Rumanians—and with their relatives, who obviously were also Rumanians.

They turned to the Manhattan phone book for American guidance in the important decision. There they found beautiful-sounding American names like Kakarakis and Rodriguez and Yee and Rosenthal and Pacini and Smith. Vladimir and Miru made lists of hundreds of names, but not one struck them as being exactly right.

Then, sipping a cup of coffee at the counter of the All-American Luncheonette and Take-Out Emporium one day, Vladimir noticed something he had never noticed before. Three out of five customers eating lunch ordered tuna fish sandwiches—some on white, some on rye, and some on rolls. Vladimir questioned the counterman about the phenomenon.

"Hey, mister, why come so many American lunch customers eating tuna fish?"

"They like it, buddy," answered the counterman.

"You make it special way, mister?" asked Vladimir.

"Naw. It's a real American food, chum. Everybody likes tuna. It's a tradition—like hot dogs and hamburgers and apple pie."

"*Everybody* like tuna? Amazing!" said Vladimir, and ordered a tuna sandwich. He liked it.

Wiping the last crumbs from his mouth, Vladimir had his great inspiration. He had found a way to keep part of his venerable old family name—Tunitsky—and make it as American as apple pie. That night Vladimir and Miru Tunitsky spent hours with their list of first names. Vladimir wanted to make sure they picked the most American names possible. In the end, it was their night-school American history book that guided them to their final choices.

"We're no back numbers, Miru, my love. These are genuine, red, white, and blues, ups-to-date USA names." Miru agreed one hundred percent.

The next week Vladimir and Miru Tunitsky went to court and legally became George Washington and Betsy Ross Tuna. When the judge asked them why they had picked that particular last name, Vladimir Tunitsky replied, "Because everybody in the USA love tuna, Mr. Judge, Your Honor. It's an all-American name. It will speed up our melting better."

"Speed up your melting?"

"Into the pot, judge, sir."

The judge smiled at the new George Washington Tuna and Betsy Ross Tuna and signed the papers.

Brenda ended her story by explaining that for as long as she had known them—which was her whole life—her grandparents had never called each other anything but Vladimir and Miru. However, they insisted that the grandchildren call them Grandpa George and Grandma Betsy.

"Didn't that confuse you when you were growing up?" I asked Brenda.

"Not really. On a scale of one to ten, the entire name issue ranks about a two."

"A two how, Brenda?" I asked.

"One being normal and ten being bizarre."

"For whom?" Brenda was not making herself clear.

"For my family, of course. How we got our family name is just about the most normal thing anyone in my family has ever done."

"Impressive!" I said.

"Embarrassing sometimes," said Brenda.

"But interesting. You actually have a family that is interesting. Do you want to trade sandwich halves?"

"What are you eating?"

"Tuna fish," I said.

"I never touch the stuff."

"I understand."

"I know." Brenda smiled at me.

Three days later—the day Brenda Tuna wore a Japanese kimono to school and was late to homeroom because she could only take tiny baby steps, being restricted by both the tightly wrapped long garment and the high wooden platform shoes— we decided to become best friends.

In honor of the occasion, Brenda chose a spectacular outfit for the following day—a Hawaiian grass skirt, a halter top, and a lei made from real flowers. Her entrance into homeroom was accompanied by music from a small tape player. For a short, shapeless, eleven-and-a-half-year-old, Brenda Tuna did a pretty mean hula. The entire class hooted and cheered.

Mr. Osgood sent Brenda straight down to the guidance office.

"You are a disturbed young woman, Tunafish," he hollered at her back as she swayed down the hall. "As for the rest of you, one more outburst like that and you'll all end up in detention for a month."

The guidance counselor sent Brenda home with a note recommending counseling. Brenda told me her mother read the note and then slipped it into the canary cage, which she happened to be cleaning. After covering the note with clean gravel, Mrs. Tuna told Brenda that it would be a good idea for Brenda to dress more conservatively when going to school—that probably too much of her skin had been showing, in noncompliance with the dress code. Mrs. Tuna advised that Brenda wear something more modest—like a sarong—if she wanted to express a tropical mood. Brenda, not caring to be sent home twice in one day, opted for a modest, flowing Indian sari.

I learned about her talk with her mother at lunch.

"She didn't get angry?" I asked in amazement.

"No, why should she?" said Brenda.

"Because you got sent home—because of the note—because of the hula skirt. None of this bothers her?"

"Why should it? My mother understands everything about me." Brenda did not say this in a happy way.

"I would really like to meet your mother, Brenda."

"Come home with me today, but don't be surprised by anything you see."

"Surprised? She sounds great!"

"I know. Sometimes I think my mother is the biggest obstacle in my life."

"That doesn't make sense." I didn't see how a great mother could be a problem.

"There's nothing to rebel against." Brenda sounded miserable.

"That's good, isn't it?"

"It's good for little kids, but a teenager needs something to push against—to disagree with—you know attitudes, behavior, unreasonable rules."

"You're not a teenager yet."

"I'm precocious. Mentally and emotionally I am years ahead of myself."

The bell rang and ended our conversation. After school we walked the three blocks to Brenda's house.

"Welcome to The Retreat," said Brenda, stopping at a yard completely hidden by a six-foot-high, wooden fence. She opened a door cut into what had looked like a solid wall.

"Oh," was all I could manage to say. "Oh!" I found myself saying it again.

"I told you the Tunas did not exactly do things in a normal

way," said Brenda. "Let's go meet my mom. She's probably throwing pots." Brenda started walking down a gravel path.

"At what?" I giggled.

Brenda gave me a funny look. I followed her slowly. About halfway to the house, I realized that my mouth was hanging open.

▽ ▽ ▽

FOUR

I GOT to understand a whole lot about Brenda Tuna the first time I visited The Retreat. You see, Brenda and I live in the town of Florence, Long Island. Not that long ago it was a perfectly fine, productive potato farm surrounded by some very pretty woods close to the Atlantic Ocean. Along came Harmon A. Harmon, real estate developer and builder of single-family houses. HAH, as he was called by his employees (behind his back, of course), bought the potato farm, the woods, the adjacent vegetable farm, and a nice strip of clean sandy beach.

Then he began building. In ten years, the wildlife, the potatoes, the vegetables, the untouched beach, and most of the trees were gone. In their place was a village, a post office, a police station, hundreds of houses, waterfront condos, three schools, and about five thousand people. Ten years after that, Florence had grown to become the number-one suburb of New York City.

Florence was not named after Florence, Italy, a very nice place, I hear. It was named after Florence Edna Harmon, HAH's wife. Brenda says that Florence, Long Island, expresses the essence of Florence Harmon, whom she refers to as FEH. Brenda has never actually met FEH in person but has observed her shopping in the expensive boutiques on Diedre Street, Florence, Long Island's main drag.

FEH shops every day. She always wears lots of jewelry—even to the supermarket—and is never without some large, expensive, and often exotic fur coat or fur cape—summer as well as winter. In the summertime, she rides around in her Mercedes-Benz with the windows rolled up and the air conditioner blasting. FEH has a special way of sliding out of her fur wrap, out of her freezing car, and into ninety-degree, muggy, unbreathable air dressed in very skimpy outfits. Brenda says FEH's car exits always remind her of a snake shedding its skin.

Brenda is very much against killing wild animals in order to make coats for the FEHs of the world. She feels that fur is much prettier on the body where it originally grew. Brenda also believes that, with few exceptions, the original four-legged fur-bearing beasts are much nicer than their successors. This is only one of the areas in which Brenda Tuna has very definite opinions.

Florence, Long Island, is a snobbish, boring, totally predictable suburb. There are neat houses surrounded by neat lawns dotted with neat landscaping consisting of neat trees and shrubs and flower beds. In the litter-free, tree-lined, neat village there are a number of stores selling expensive clothing, jewelry, and gift items. There are four restaurants specializing in fancy fad-food—like croissants and quiches and pasta salads. There are two ice-cream parlors where coffee costs a dollar fifty a cup and sundaes start at four dollars. There is no McDonald's or Burger King in downtown Florence. The cheapest hamburger you can buy costs four dollars and ninety-five cents—without fries.

On the edge of town, there is a large, climate-controlled mall with marble walkways, fountains, trees, and caged songbirds. It has earned the National Mall Cleanliness Award four years in a row. That's where the kids buy their designer sneakers, designer pants, designer shirts, and designer underwear—which you have to have in order to undress in the gym locker room without getting teased.

Brenda says that appearances are the most important thing in Florence. She makes her mother drive her inland to the next town so she can buy her socks and underwear at Sears. I once saw her spend a whole afternoon carefully cutting labels, swans, horses, alligators, and other status symbols off a bunch of clothing she'd received from relatives for her birthday. As she worked, she lectured me on the subject of the Great Conspiracy of Manufacturers. Brenda claimed the Conspiracy had succeeded in its dastardly goal of forcing people to overpay for what amounted to the privilege of advertising the very products they bought. While she talked, she made little holes and snags in her new wardrobe. Brenda said she didn't care as long as her new clothes wound up being as anonymous as her old ones.

Closing the fence gate behind us that first day really did transport us out of Florence. In the middle of the world's neatest, most conventional, world-class uptight town, the Tuna family house sat in an unmowed meadow. White board fencing divided what should have been a lawn into two small pastures. In one, three sheep were munching on a pile of hay. In the other, a goat and two geese seemed to be eating weeds.

"Sheep?" I said, finally able to speak. We were standing on a path between the two pastures.

"Marigold, Rose, and Petunia. They belong to my mother. She weaves."

"Goat?" I said, sounding more and more like a two-year-old.

"Lillybelle. She's mine. She's a milking goat. Come, Lillybelle!" Brenda called, and the goat came trotting over to us.

Brenda scratched her between the ears while Lillybelle tried to take a bite out of Brenda's biology book.

"Geese?" I began turning red with embarrassment. The more I stood there, the more it felt like we were no longer in Florence.

"You having some trouble with all this, India?" asked Brenda.

I nodded. My voice seemed to have left me.

"It gets me, too, even though I've lived here for years. It's an illusion—the feeling of being out in the countryside. Not mowing helps, because it gives the wildflowers a chance to grow. Do you like it?"

"Yes," I whispered. I could finally speak a little. I was relieved.

We began walking again. I followed Brenda around the house, past a couple of beehives, a big vegetable garden, and into a small orchard.

"Doesn't it seem like we have acres and acres of land?" asked Brenda.

I had just been wondering how the Tunas had found such a large tract of land practically in the center of town.

"Actually, it's only an acre and a half. My father is an expert in space planning. He's working on a book about suburban homesteading."

"Your father's a writer?" Brenda and I had never gotten around to discussing what our parents did.

"Not exactly. He owns a costume-supply business in Manhattan—rentals and sales."

"That's where you get all your school clothing?"

"Yes. I tell him what I am interested in, and he brings it home from his warehouse. Sometimes he surprises me and arrives with his own idea of interesting clothing."

"Your father dresses in costumes, too?" I wondered just how weird the Tunas were.

"Not for him, India. He invents costume ideas for *me*."

We had walked through the little orchard and were standing in front of what had once been a garage. The lower level was now fixed up as a barn. Brenda walked past some animal pens and stopped at the foot of a ladderlike staircase.

"Brenda, are you telling me that your father helps you choose strange costumes to wear to school?"

"Costumes are his life, or so he claims," answered Brenda as she began to climb the steps.

"But he's a father! He's supposed to be conventional, isn't he? He lives in Florence! I mean, you get *both* your parents' approval for doing bizarre things. How come you're so lucky?"

"Lucky? *Lucky?* Are you crazy? It's terrible! My life is a disaster! I am an individual. A bona fide, genuine, pure-to-the-core *individual*. I am a teenager. . . . Don't you understand?"

"Almost a teenager," I reminded the gesticulating Brenda, who was balancing on a step halfway up the steep flight.

"Okay. Almost. I am ready to rebel—to soar—to express my independence—to test my abilities in the hard, cruel world—to grow—to experience—to . . . to . . ."

"So," I interrupted, "nothing is stopping you. Nothing and nobody gets in your way. What's your big problem?"

"I was sure *you* would understand, you, India Ink Teidlebaum, my best friend in the entire world." Brenda sat on a step and stared sadly down at me, shaking her head.

"What don't I understand? Tell me. Fast." Brenda had given herself the advantage. Capturing an audience seemed to be something she did naturally, without thinking. I was holding on to the ladder steps and leaning back so I could see her face, and my hands were beginning to cramp.

24

"Oh, sorry, India. Let's get to the top." Once on the landing, Brenda finished her explanation.

"I can't just rebel in a vacuum. I can't break away if nothing is holding me back. I am cursed with totally agreeable, offbeat, accepting, understanding, helpful parents."

"You're kidding. That's ridiculous, Brenda. Any kid would trade all his or her worldly possessions for one month in a family like yours."

"Wrong. Wrong. *Wrong!* Look, the only way you're ever going to understand is to see the Tuna family in action. Let's introduce you to my mother."

"Fine with me, but I think you're nuts, Brenda."

"You'll see for yourself," Brenda grumbled, and led me into Mrs. Tuna's pottery studio.

▽ ▽ ▽

FIVE

THE first thing that impressed me about Brenda's mother was her size. She was and is a tall, large, shapely woman. By Florence standards, she is fat. I only mention this because, after boutiques and salad restaurants, the most popular type of business in town happens to be body reshaping establishments. There are three elegant exercise salons on Diedre Street, two plainer health clubs in the mall, and at least four similar places scattered around town. They are all busy all of the time.

Both country clubs have workout rooms, and for those shy, rich people unwilling to leave their homes to exercise in public, there is always Ira's Shapemobile standing by—seven days a week. Ira guarantees that within twenty-four hours of your phone call to his special emergency number—OFF-FATT—he will have an exercise instructor and one of his fully equipped minigym trucks in your driveway.

Thinness is a way of life in Florence. It's the only place I've ever been where you can buy bumper stickers that say, BETTER DEAD THAN FAT! Weekend mornings, regardless of weather conditions, hundreds of joggers and runners rush out of their houses and take to the streets. Their presence makes driving a car or riding a bicycle almost impossible.

Kids who are even slightly chubby have a rough time—even in grade school. I am an expert on the topic because I am, what my mother calls, a stocky person. Brenda politely calls me an endomorph, which is a word from anthropology meaning short, stocky human being. My gym teacher calls me blubber butt, which is a nasty dig. Boys simply don't notice me. Nobody uses the word *fat*. I think calling someone fat out loud in downtown Florence would probably be punished by a jail term or, at least, banishment.

So, in the middle of conventional Florence with its manicured lawns and its mania for thin, my new friend, Brenda Tuna, lived on a weedy, rocky, natural-looking minifarm—with a very chunky mother.

The second thing I noticed about Mrs. Tuna was the way she was dressed. She was wearing overalls, a work shirt, and work boots—practical clothing for a potter but unheard of covering for an adult female resident of Florence.

Mrs. Tuna is the only adult I have ever met in Florence who uses the word *fat* as a description and not a curse. She is a fine woman, a good friend, but, according to Brenda, a lousy mother for a teenager. That first day we sat snacking on milk and cookies while I witnessed this exchange between the two Tunas.

"Mother, I am going to rebel. It's time."

"That's nice, dear. I think such a decision shows a deep understanding of your own psyche."

"Stop it, Mother!"

"Stop what, dear?"

"Stop agreeing with me."

"Are you saying you need conflict in your home life in order to rebel with meaning?"

"Yes. I want you to become a better mother. Make an unreasonable rule. Force your old-fashioned values on me."

"I'll try, dear, but I don't think I have any that could really be termed *old-fashioned.*"

"Can't you disagree with me—just once? Try it, Mom. Disagree! You're making me crazy with understanding."

Mrs. Tuna smiled and looked lovingly at Brenda. "I'll work on it, dear. Would you girls like some ice cream?"

"I give up," moaned Brenda.

That was the beginning of my years of hanging out at the Tuna house where, in time, I learned to use a potter's wheel, shear a sheep, pluck down from a struggling goose, and milk a goat. I also learned how to have an interesting conversation at a dinner table.

During our first semester in junior high, the Tunas invited my family to The Retreat for dinner. I was excited and nervous about the two families meeting.

"What if they hate each other?" I asked Brenda.

"Impossible," insisted Brenda.

"Smoke is going to do something gross at dinner—I know it," I complained.

"So what. He's a kid."

"Rain might become obnoxious."

"That's to be expected. See you tonight," said Brenda.

Smoke didn't do one disgusting thing during the meal and actually had a real conversation with Mr. Tuna. After dinner, at Mrs. Tuna's invitation, my mother sat down at the big loom in the living room and worked on the cloth Mrs. Tuna was weaving.

"I didn't know you could weave, Mom." I was very surprised.

My mother laughed. "I'm a little rusty. The last thing I wove was Smoke's baby blanket—just before we left the commune."

"Mother, *please!*" Rain was bugged. For years she had been trying desperately to get my mother to swear a solemn oath never to mention our hippie beginnings in front of any resident of Florence.

"Be quiet, Rain. The Tunas don't care where we lived before we came here." My father was sitting on the floor in front of the fireplace playing chess with Mr. Tuna.

Rain got up and stomped into the bathroom, where she sulked for the rest of our visit. On the way home she announced that she couldn't stand The Retreat, Mrs. Tuna's size, or The Philosopher. She said they embarrassed her, made her uncomfortable, made her feel "yicky." She thought that we, her family, all acted like jerks, and she couldn't understand why we didn't socialize with proper people who sat in chairs and dressed up when they entertained.

"Before you ruin our good mood, Rain, dear, I suggest you shut up." My mother's face was smiling. Her voice was not. Rain shut up.

"When we were young, your father and I enjoyed the idea of being free spirits much more than we enjoyed the actual life.

28

Did you know that, India?"

"No, Mom. I always wondered why we wound up in Florence."

"Well, to be truthful, we felt both awkward and more than a little out of place much of the time we were trying to be children of nature. For us, living in tents and on communes was an adventure—more a vacation from real life than it was a commitment to a new kind of society we wanted to help design."

"Your mother's right. One day we realized that the adventure had worn thin. We had three small children and a life to build. Now your mother and I are comfortable in Florence. I like my job. I find it challenging. I will never regret a minute of our lives as hippies, but this is our world now."

We pulled into our driveway. Rain slammed into the house. My father picked up Smoke, who had fallen asleep. "I'll put him to bed," he whispered.

My mother put her arm around me. "India, I'm sorry that I gave you a name you hate. It seemed so beautiful and appropriate at the time. Perhaps we can have it changed legally to something more conventional such as Jane or Susan or . . ."

"It's okay, Mom. I've decided I like my name after all. Brenda says it expresses my uniqueness and that I will never get absorbed by the milling masses."

"Milling masses? The Philosopher certainly turns a phrase now and then. I'm so happy that you like your name."

"Me, too." I hugged my mother. "Was the sky really special the night I was born?"

"It was spectacular."

"Do you think Rain will ever like the Tunas?" I asked.

"No. She's too inflexible. Don't let it bother you."

I never have.

ЅIX

AS it turned out, my sister Rain's narrow view of life was typical. In that first month of junior high, Brenda and I had discovered that hardly anyone admired true uniqueness.

Brenda had been under a great deal of pressure, for a seventh grader. Osgood, teacher of English; Meyer, teacher of math; Ballard, teacher of French; Morton, teacher of gym—in fact, the entire faculty, except Ms. Wilson, teacher of art, had been on Brenda's case. It got so she couldn't walk down the hallway between classes without some teacher stopping to question her or lecture her about her outfits. After a week they all knew her name. Brenda was arbitrarily sent to the guidance office for "attire" at least once a day. One teacher called her a "disruptive influence." Another called her "nuts." Brenda got to know all the guidance counselors, the school psychologist, and the principal during the first few weeks of school.

"I am a true individual. I join no movement. I follow no clique. I hurt no person. I insist upon my rights. . . ." We would hear her voice ringing in the empty hallways as some teacher dragged her to her daily session with the guidance department.

The kids were hardly divided about Brenda. Most thought she was a fruitcake. A few were afraid of her. Even I began to have my doubts. I didn't want to hurt her feelings, but I had to confront my friend. Finally I got up my courage and cornered her.

"Why do you do it?" I asked.

"Really, India, you of all people," she snapped at me.

"Maybe I'm a little slow, but I am your friend. Explain why you're putting yourself through all this."

Brenda looked bugged. Then she looked embarrassed. "I'm stuck," she admitted.

"What do you mean, stuck?"

"I'm stuck. I dressed up the first day of school as a joke, but Osgood was such a creep that I did it again—and again. Then the other teachers got on my case, and I couldn't back down. It was a matter of honor. I thought I'd get some support from my fellow students, but I have simply become an object of ridicule."

"That's not true," I insisted. "A whole bunch of kids admire your . . . your . . ." I searched for the right word.

"Stubbornness? Independence? Individuality? Uniqueness?" suggested Brenda.

"Right. All those things."

"Hah! How many would you guess admire me, India? Five? Six? Maybe ten out of hundreds?"

"More. Many more," I lied.

"Let's face it, India. I'm famous—not loved. I'm the school eccentric. I can accept that. But as a person I have a reputation to uphold. The eyes of Florence Junior High are upon me. I can't simply give in to Osgood and the rest of them. Unfortunately, I've painted myself into a corner. I want out, but I'm stuck."

"How stuck are you? Are you stuck like epoxy or a peel-away sticker?" I tried to keep it light. My friend was in trouble, and I couldn't think of anything helpful to say to her.

"That's IT!" she shouted.

"What's it?" I asked.

"You've really helped me, India. You're a genius."

"I didn't say anything," I insisted.

"See you in school tomorrow." Brenda walked away from my house muttering to herself, "Unstuck, of course. Peel off the sticker. . . ."

The next day Brenda sauntered into homeroom wearing jeans and a shirt and took her usual seat. Mr. Osgood smirked at her. Brenda smiled radiantly up at him. Finally he mentioned the lack of a costume.

"Decided to buckle under and conform, Miss Tuna? Let this be an example for the rest of you ingrates. In any difference of opinion between the faculty and the students, the faculty will prevail. Rules will be followed. Standards will be met. Isn't that so, Miss Tuna?"

"I don't understand what you are talking about, sir," answered Brenda politely.

"Your lack of bizarre and disruptive costume, Miss Tuna." Mr. Osgood was annoyed.

"Costume? What costume are you referring to, Mr. Osgood? I'm wearing perfectly conventional kid clothing." Brenda was now giving Osgood her serious, concerned look.

"Don't confuse the issue and don't pretend to be stupider than you are. You have obviously folded under pressure to conform to standard patterns of behavior."

"I don't think I'm stupid, sir. So far this year I have received straight A's in all my classes—including yours. Why are you calling me stupid, Mr. Osgood?"

"You are dodging the issue, young lady. Admit that you have, for the first time, appeared in school attired in the sloppy but normal clothing of a seventh grader."

"What else should I wear to school, sir? I really don't grasp what you are trying to get me to say."

The exchange went on for at least ten minutes. The class listened in amazed silence. Mr. Osgood was furious. Brenda never stopped smiling. She was literally saved by the bell.

"If you peel away a sticker, it's as if it had never been there, right, India?" Brenda whispered as we left homeroom.

"Except if it leaves behind those little bits of glue you can never remove," I answered.

"Don't be such a naysayer," said Brenda. "I'm unstuck. No trace of my costumes exists, except in the minds of the people— and people have a way of forgetting things."

"Maybe," I said.

As far as I know, Brenda Tuna never admitted to anyone, ever, that she had worn costumes to school that entire first month of seventh grade. The kids decided that the entire costume caper was an elaborate trick Brenda had planned to best Mr. Osgood and the other adults in the school. Brenda became something of an instant school legend. She managed to stay in the limelight all through seventh and eighth grades.

Unfortunately, her fame taught me another important lesson. Celebrity is not necessarily the same as popularity.

"Don't worry about it, India," Brenda would say after I pointed out that simple fact to her for the hundredth time. "I've got a plan. It will all work out when we're ninth graders. We're going to run this school. How does student council president sound?"

"How does school principal sound?" I would grumble.

"Don't be sarcastic, India. You'll see. Ninth grade will be our year of glory."

I was just starting to believe her when it was announced that, because of a population shift, the school board had reorganized the schools in Florence. Beginning the following year, Florence Junior High would have only two grades, seventh and eighth. The ninth grade would be moving on to the high school as a traditional high-school freshman class.

"You tricked me," I accused my friend.

"Come on, India, be fair." Brenda laughed.

"Okay, so it wasn't your fault. How can you be so happy?

Next year we'll be starting all over again from the bottom. Where was our year of glory? We were robbed."

"Think of the opportunities. New horizons. New goals. A chance to shape the destiny of a larger, more important educational institution." Brenda was getting worked up.

"Maybe we should just quietly ease into school this time around," I suggested. "Let's find out how things work at the high school before we start to shape its destiny."

Brenda pretended she hadn't heard me and changed the subject. "My family is leaving on a camping trip the day after school is out."

"How long will you be away?" I asked.

"The whole summer. My mother says you're invited to join us. Think your folks will let you come?"

"Why not? Where are you going?" I asked. Suddenly school didn't seem that important.

"The Amazon," said Brenda.

"Jungle?"

"River and jungle." Brenda didn't seem to be joking.

"I'll ask," I said, knowing in advance it was hopeless.

"Man-eating fish," said my mother.

"Man-eating crocodiles," said my father.

"Man-eating snakes," said Rain.

"Man-eating men," said Smoke.

"I'm a young woman, not a man," I said. "I'll be safe."

Smoke giggled. Rain sniggered. My parents ignored me.

"Why couldn't they go camping someplace less dangerous?" said my mother.

"Like the Florida Everglades," suggested Smoke.

"Good idea," said Rain. "That would eliminate the man-eating men."

"And the fish," added Smoke. "All India would have to

worry about would be snakes, alligators, and deadly insects."

"There are no deadly insects in the Everglades." I was getting angry.

"Well, how about the quicksand?" said Smoke as he slid off his chair and pretended he was being sucked into the earth.

"I want to thank you two for helping me out," I snarled.

"Don't mention it," said Rain.

"Likewise," said Smoke, wiping make-believe quicksand off his face.

The Tunas were not about to change their plans to suit my family. I stayed home, worried about ninth grade, and watched my face break out. Brenda flew off to experience the natural wonders and dangers of the Amazon River Basin. Some people have all the luck—and that summer I was not one of them.

▽ ▽ ▽

SEVEN

BRENDA and I had just returned from our first miserable day as freshmen at Florence Senior High. We were sitting in the Tuna living room eating homemade whole wheat pizza.

"Thank you for not making a spectacle of yourself today, Brenda."

"Stuff it," said Brenda, scratching an insect bite. I had rarely seen Brenda in a worse mood.

"Thanks, anyway."

"If I had known Osgood was being moved to the senior high and would wind up being my English teacher again, I would have planned something diabolical."

"Too late now."

35

"It's never too late," said Brenda.

"Yes, it is. Besides, why waste your genius on a jerk like Osgood when our entire future is at stake." Sometimes flattery worked with Brenda.

"Nice try, India. And how was your first glorious day of high school?"

"Not great," I mumbled.

"I've always known you wouldn't like anonymity."

"That's not it," I said. "I don't care if nobody knows me. I just don't like being at the bottom of the social order."

"You care. Every freshman cares. We just have to face reality, India, and learn to live with it. We're never going to be cheerleaders."

"What are you talking about, Brenda? Who wants to be a cheerleader? And why are you changing the subject?"

"I'm not. Your unhappiness is a simple, common symptom of adolescence."

"You're not exactly laughing with joy yourself."

"Don't get me off the track, India. In a place like Florence, all girls—secretly if not obviously—want to be cheerleaders." Brenda began to perk up.

"That's idiotic."

"No, it isn't. Examine the facts, India. How are cheerleaders perceived?"

"What do you mean by *perceived*?"

"I mean how are they seen rather than what are they actually. Let's consider just the ones in Florence."

I thought for a minute and answered, "Cute."

"That's perception number one. Cheerleaders are cute—bouncy, smiling, squeaky-clean, adorable cute."

"Isn't it true?"

"Hah! Even you have been bamboozled. No, it is often not

36

true, but nobody notices. Cheerleaders spend most of their time perfecting their image by smiling, jumping in the air, waving their arms, cheering, and looking likable. In the end, the image covers up the reality."

"What about their faces? They are, too, always cute!" I was sure I had Brenda on that point.

"Double hah! You have been brainwashed. In places like Florence, the faces are not so much cute as standardized."

"What does that mean?"

"Only people with certain types of faces are chosen for the squads. There have been cases where fine athletes with pep and charm have not been voted onto the cheerleading squads because of their nonconforming faces."

"Brenda . . ."

"No, listen to me. Did you ever compare the noses of the fifteen junior varsity cheerleaders to the noses of the sixteen senior varsity cheerleaders?"

"Of course not."

"Buttons. Small, turned-up buttons."

"What are you talking about?"

"Button noses. Tiny, little, turned-up button noses—all of them. Do you think that's coincidence?"

"It has to be."

"You mean you believe that the only girls in an entire town who are athletically good enough to qualify for the cheerleading squads have button noses? Pretty naive, India."

"Okay. I see your point, I think. No, I don't. Why are their noses important?"

"Who is to say that small, button noses are the cutest noses of all? Why, those who already have such noses. Who elects new cheerleaders? The old cheerleaders, of course. It's noses perpetuating noses."

"Come on, Brenda."

"You come on. It's true. The old cheerleaders pick new ones who look like themselves—because then there is no doubt in anyone's mind what cute is. Cheerleaders are cute, therefore button noses are cute, therefore cheerleaders are cute."

"That's a circle. It doesn't make sense."

"Sense has nothing to do with images. What's another perception involving cheerleaders?"

"They're popular."

"Bingo! Cute and popular—the secret dream of every teen-age girl. Become a cheerleader and be cute and popular and *well known* by all because that's what cheerleaders are. Unfortunately, the only way you can do this is to be a carbon copy of the already existing Florence cheerleaders. Those who don't quite make it become pom-pom girls. Then there are the twirlers and then there are the rest of us."

"How come you're so sure of this, Brenda?"

"I've been observing. Out of approximately six hundred high-school girls, we are just about the only two who have never practiced."

"When did you do all this observing? We've only been in school for one day. Practiced for what?"

"Sometimes I think you are unconscious, India. What did you think was going on in the halls, on the school buses, in town, in gym, during lunch, before school, in the mall, all summer . . . ?"

"You weren't here all summer."

"Details. I've been around other summers."

"Not really," I insisted.

"Well, part of other summers. Don't you want me to explain your depression to you?"

"I can hardly wait. Get to the point. What goings-on do

you think you've seen?"

"The arm waving, the chanting of cheers, the squat jumps, the cartwheels, the leaps—did you think everyone but us was having a strange kind of fit? They're *practicing cheering.*" Brenda looked smug.

"Oh, that."

"Oh, that? *Oh, that?* Don't you see what it all means?"

"No." It bugged me when Brenda was able to back up one of her strange theories with facts.

"Do you really think all of those girls want to be cheerleaders for the athletic gratification of the sport?"

"I never thought about it at all."

"They want to be cheerleaders so they can be cute and *popular!* They want to be part of the in-group. They want to hang around with the football and basketball players. They want to walk down the halls and have everyone know they are cheerleaders. If they happen to be good, all the better. If the squad wins a regional championship—great. But what is really important is the fact of being popular—of being a cheerleader."

"Doesn't popular mean that everyone likes you?" I asked.

"Not in school."

"What are you talking about, Brenda?"

"Definitions of words depend upon context sometimes. Junior and senior high schools are special contexts. Didn't you learn anything in junior high?"

"No need to get nasty, Brenda."

"Sorry. In school, popular means being part of a special clique that is *perceived* as being above all other cliques in school."

"*Above?* You mean, better than?"

"Yes."

"That's disgusting."

"That's traditional. For example, the popular kids in our

39

schools hang around with each other, date each other, go only to each others' houses and parties. They sit near each other in class, eat with each other in the cafeteria, and generally regard the rest of the school as being slightly less human than their own little group. It's very tribal."

"But all cliques behave that way."

"But only one is perceived by most others as actually being better, superior, to be envied."

"You're exaggerating, Brenda."

"Not very much."

"How do the rest of the kids really feel about the *popular* kids?"

"You're getting sharp, India. The majority of kids often resent, are jealous of, and gossip about the *popular* kids. At the same time they will vote for them in elections and wish in their secret hearts they were one of them. It's a very complicated adolescent set of feelings."

"You mean the twelve hundred or so of us inferior types are doomed to feel we are outsiders for our entire school careers?" I was getting more depressed. Brenda's ideas sometimes did that to me.

"Well, a whole lot of kids spend their adolescence bemoaning the fact they are not one of the *popular* kids."

"And the rest?"

"Private, occasional, secret wishes aside, they go about the business of growing up. Some go on to achieve genuine, deserved, honest-to-goodness popularity—which, for your information, means favored, approved, or beloved by the people."

"I would rather be that someday. Which brings me to a point—why are we talking about this?"

"Because we're going to have to choose a different area of interest in order to make our mark in high school."

"Different from what?"

"Cheerleading, India. Cheerleading."

"But I wasn't interested in cheerleading in the first place."

"Let's not go in circles. We need an after-school activity."

"Why?"

"Because hanging around with nobody but each other is going to get boring after a while. Let's face it, India. However you define it, at this moment, we couldn't even be elected officers of the nerd club."

"Nerd club?"

"A figure of speech."

The following Monday we joined both the school newspaper and the drama club. Three days after that, Brenda quit the drama club to protest my being assigned to the stage crew.

"But I can't act, Brenda. I don't mind."

"There is no potential glory in building sets and moving furniture around, India."

"I like building sets. I don't want glory."

"Are you telling me that you are going to stay in this shortsighted organization after I have given up my acting career for your sake?"

"You just didn't like the part you got, Brenda."

"How can you accuse me of such a low motive? I'm hurt." Brenda actually squeezed a tear from one eye.

"That's very good, Brenda. Okay. I'll quit the club. Now what?" I had lied to Brenda about enjoying my stage-crew work. Quitting was a relief.

"Did you really like being on the stage crew?" Brenda asked, wiping away her tear.

"Sure."

"Isn't it wonderful how best friends make sacrifices for each other," said Brenda.

"Wonderful."

"We'll concentrate on becoming journalists, because the written word is much more important than the spoken word," announced Brenda.

"I'm not so sure that's true these days, Brenda. How about television?"

"Why quibble, India? For our purposes, here at Florence Senior High School, the written word is going to become all-important. We're going to take over the school newspaper and ultimately influence the entire school. We might never become popular, but I can guarantee you that we will become notorious!" Brenda smiled and tucked a pencil behind her ear.

"We?"

"You're my best friend, aren't you? I wouldn't dream of leaving you behind to wallow in mediocrity."

"Brenda, I think I should remind you, we're only copygirls on the paper."

"For now. I have plans. I have foresight. I have confidence. Trust me, India, trust me."

"I only have one question, Brenda."

"Shoot."

"Is *notorious* the word you meant to use?"

"Certainly."

"Too bad."

▽ ▽ ▽

EIGHT

WE headed directly for the office of the *Florence Weekly Crier* where we found six bored-looking upperclassmen lounging around. They paid no attention to us as we entered.

"Let's not bother with this today, Brenda," I whispered.

"Now is as good a time as any to begin our new careers," said Brenda. Then, using the same volume she had successfully used on stage, she boomed, "A better name for this rag would be the *Florence Weekly Flounder*—or maybe the *Florence Weekly Fluke.*"

I wanted to die. "What are you doing, Brenda?" I whispered.

"Moving up the corporate ladder," she answered.

"Who are those children?" asked one of the lounging girls.

"Juvenile delinquent freshmen, I suppose," said another kid.

"Copygirls," said a boy, pushing past us into the room. "I signed them on a few days ago." I recognized Lawrence Snyder, the kid we had spoken to on Monday.

"You must be slipping, Lawrence. Didn't you explain things to them?" said a bored-looking, perfectly groomed girl who was sitting on a desk, filing her nails.

"There's nothing to explain." Lawrence motioned to us to sit down.

"Is, too," insisted the girl.

"Explain what?" asked Brenda.

"No freshmen allowed." The girl held her hand at arm's length and examined her nails.

"If you bit your nails, you'd have more time for developing your mind and doing useful work," said Brenda.

"I beg your pardon." The girl looked down her nose at Brenda.

"You can't have a no-freshmen rule. It's illegal," said Brenda.

"Well, then, freshmen aren't allowed to be reporters," said a boy, looking up from the magazine he was reading.

"Let's get out of here, Brenda." I tugged at Brenda's sleeve.

Naturally Brenda ignored me. "You can't restrict who works here or what they do. This is a school organization supported by school funds, which are provided by the taxation of citizens." Brenda's voice was carrying into the hallway. A crowd had begun to gather. Lawrence closed the office door.

"Can't you get her out of here, Lawrence?" another kid complained.

"I'm editor-in-chief, not a bouncer. Besides, she's right. Anyone can join the staff of the *Crier*. You jerks are prime examples of that fact."

"Power has gone to your head. We should never have elected you editor-in chief," said the girl with the perfect nails.

"You didn't elect me. The real staff did," said Lawrence. "If I recall correctly, all of you voted for yourselves. One vote each."

"What's going to happen to our extracurricular credit for college if you give our jobs away to babies?" A boy who had appeared to be asleep spoke in a petulant voice.

"Don't you worry your indolent little heads about any of this. Your jobs are safe. You can go now. It's time for the rest of us to do some newspaper work." Lawrence opened the door. The six loafers left.

As soon as they were gone, the room began to fill up with other kids. Each one got right to work, and in five minutes the office of the *Florence Weekly Crier* looked and sounded like the city room of a real newspaper.

"What was that all about?" asked Brenda.

"As you so aptly reminded us, anyone can join any club or organization. Those kids show up once a week, sit around for a half hour shooting off their mouths, and then leave."

"Why do they do it?" I asked.

"So they can list the school newspaper as an activity on college applications. We don't object. In fact, we even occasionally vote to give them titles—reporter, feature writer—whatever they want to be called."

"Why?" asked Brenda.

"You should also be asking when, where, who, how, . . ." said a kid with owllike eyeglasses.

"Cute," said Brenda. "Is anyone going to answer my question?"

"Pushy freshman, isn't she? I think I remember her from junior high," said a girl.

"Me, too. Isn't she Brenda Tuna?"

"And her sidekick, what's-her-name?"

"I'm leaving," I announced.

"They're just teasing you," said Lawrence. "They always get a little rough with each other on Bimbo Day."

"India Ink something or other," said a boy.

"Teidlebaum," I said.

"Right," said the boy.

"Of course I'm right. It's my name."

"One never knows on Bimbo Day." The boy went back to work.

"We try to avoid the parasites," said a girl, "but somehow we always run into them."

"To answer your question, we tolerate the bimbos because we have to. We give them titles, which appear on the masthead, and the newspaper looks as if it has a larger, more active staff than it does. This secures a healthy share of the club budget money," Lawrence explained. "Now it's my turn. Is it customary for you to insult organizations you join?"

"Oh, you heard," said Brenda.

"What did she say?" asked a kid.

45

"I said that it would be more accurate to call this newspaper the *Florence Weekly Flounder* or the *Florence Weekly Fluke*," said Brenda.

A couple of kids giggled. No one seemed upset at Brenda's remark.

"Why?" asked Lawrence.

"It's boring. It's pointless. It's mostly a bulletin board for school events, fluffed out by a couple of well-written but boring feature articles every week."

"It's a school newspaper," said a girl. "What do you expect?"

"Social conscience. Curiosity. Exploration of the burning issues of our time," answered Brenda.

There were loud guffaws from all over the office.

"If we did that, they'd close us down," said Lawrence.

"They wouldn't dare. Freedom of the press is a basic right in this country," argued Brenda.

"This isn't the country. It's Florence Senior High School."

"But aren't you bored?" asked Brenda.

"We've learned to put together a paper," said a girl.

"And to write news articles," said another.

Then there was a short silence. From a corner of the room someone said, "Yes."

"Deadly bored."

"Painfully bored."

"Right."

Soon everyone was joining in.

"I told you that kid was trouble. I can see my whole life changing. Welcome, Brenda Tuna and India Ink Teidlebaum. My name is Kether."

"I'm Ben."

"Sue." They all introduced themselves.

"And what do you think of your friend's comments?" asked Lawrence.

"As Kether said, where Brenda treads, trouble follows, but I happen to agree with her."

"Any ideas about how to change things?" he asked us.

"Naturally," said Brenda. "But first I want you to promote both of us to reporters."

"Why not? We all do everything around here, anyway."

Brenda told the staff of the *Florence Weekly Crier* all about an idea she had for a schoolwide exposé.

"That is not a first-class idea," insisted Ken, a senior staff member.

"At least it's an idea," said Kether.

"But she's just a kid. A freshman. How can we trust her to know what she's talking about?"

"And she wants to do the major investigative work with India. Neither one knows what she's doing."

"Do any of us? Besides, they're best suited for this particular job. Brenda explained that to us," Lawrence said, backing Brenda up.

"And you believe her?"

"And can you stand the thought of another year of writing nothing but articles about sporting events and school plays?" asked Lawrence.

In the end, the staff of the *Crier* voted nine to two in favor of Brenda's idea.

"We're on our way," said a gleeful Brenda as we walked home.

"But where will we wind up?" I asked.

"In the limelight, of course."

"Infamous?"

"Perhaps."

"You are a dangerous friend, Brenda."

Brenda giggled.

▽ ▽ ▽

NINE

THE next day, before school, Brenda presented me with a tape recorder and a bagful of blank tapes.

"We'll start at lunch, India," she announced.

"Start what?"

"Don't be dense. Investigating."

"You mean spying."

"Spies spy. Reporters investigate. We are reporters."

I couldn't concentrate on anything all morning. By lunchtime I was a nervous wreck.

"I'm a nervous wreck," I said to Brenda as I headed for the sandwich line.

"Didn't you bring your lunch?" asked Brenda.

"I never bring my lunch."

"It's essential to my plan. I thought you might forget so I brought this." Brenda handed me a brown bag.

"You never told me to bring lunch. Did your mother make this sandwich?" I had visions of smelly goat cheese and bean sprouts covered with organic mayonnaise all crushed between two thick slices of tooth-breaking, whole-grain bread.

"Don't worry, I made it. It's peanut butter and jelly."

"Jelly? In your house?"

"It's sugarless. Now let's sit down before all the seats are gone."

That began our week of spying.

On the surface, Brenda's plan was simple. Each of us would pick a lunch table reserved by custom for the popular kids and occupy one seat at it. Actually, Brenda was to sit with the most popular kids and I was to join the overflow, which included some of the second-string popular kids—the ones who got invited to movies and parties if any of the first-string kids couldn't make it. Once in the midst of such greatness, we were to place our tape recorders on the tables, turn them on, and sit quietly while recording.

I had reservations about this plan. "They will make me eat the tape," I had insisted.

"Don't be silly. They're not a violent bunch. Take my word for it, India, nothing will happen to you." Brenda sounded totally confident—but she always sounded that way even when she was one hundred percent wrong.

Despite my fears, I found myself easing into a place at the table. I opened my lunch, placed the tape recorder in front of me. turned it on, and waited.

"Hey, do we have the wrong table?" boomed a large, muscled boy as he swung his leg over the bench, crashed his loaded tray onto the table, and sat down.

"Naw," said his companion, checking the nearest tables, "I don't think so. Maybe she's lost. You lost, kid?"

"Are you speaking to me?" I asked.

"Are you speaking to *her*?" asked a pretty girl joining us. She delicately placed her sparsely filled tray between the trays of the two boys and sat down. "Go away, little girl. This is *our* table."

Remembering Brenda's instructions, I didn't respond. I took a bite of my sandwich and stared right past the girl. I could see Brenda's table filling up. There seemed to be an argument going on. Everyone was involved except Brenda.

49

"Incredible," I mumbled.

"She spoke," said a new arrival—a very blond senior wearing her pom-pom-girl sweater.

"Why is she sitting here?"

"There won't be enough room at the table for all of us if she stays."

"Let's move."

"Why should we move? It's our table. Always has been."

"Make her move, please." A girl batted her eyelashes at one of the larger goons.

"I'm not allowed to use violence off the playing field this year." The goon was grinning at the girl.

"Who says?"

"Coach."

"Not fair," said the girl. "I'm sure Coach didn't mean for you to let some kid ruin lunch for us."

"Leave him alone, Andrea," demanded one of the other big boys. "If you get him to fight, our entire playing season will be ruined. Besides, you're asking a two-hundred-pound senior boy to physically assault a small freshman girl. That's a little extreme, isn't it?"

"Maybe. Then what should we do?"

"Ignore her."

"Ignore her?"

"Pretend she's not here. She'll go away after a while."

"What about *that*?" asked another girl, pointing to my tape recorder.

"Looks like she forgot to bring her earphones."

"Why is the tape spinning then?"

"Maybe she's a little slow."

Each new arrival at the table was told to ignore me. This helped solve their space problem. Since I wasn't really there, they didn't have to leave room for me. In a few minutes I was crushed between two of the larger boys. I couldn't even move my arms to eat my lunch. I sat quietly, listened, and observed.

"There is no blood circulating in my arms, Brenda," I complained as we left the cafeteria.

"Give me the tape, India. My plan worked, didn't it?"

"Don't you care that I have no feeling in my upper limbs? Well, at least it's over." I handed Brenda the tape recorder.

"No, keep the machine for tomorrow," she said. "Just give me the tape."

"What's happening tomorrow?" I pretended not to know.

"Stop pretending, India. We have to investigate for at least a week or our results will be meaningless."

"Who cares?" I was not in a good mood.

"Don't you want justice done?"

"Justice?"

"Justice."

What was done depends upon your point of view. We spent four more lunch hours recording the conversations of the popular kids. As far as they were concerned, we did not exist, so they talked freely.

"Enlightening," said Brenda after listening to my last tape.

"I wouldn't go that far," I said.

"Mind if I write this story, India?" asked Brenda.

"Be my guest. You don't even have to mention my name in it." I knew where Brenda was headed and wanted to go in another direction.

"Nonsense. Without you, this investigation would have been impossible."

"If you blow my cover, I'll be of less use to you on future investigations." I hoped that would deflect Brenda.

"You have a point there. But I suspect you are simply lapsing into your old, shy ways. No, India, you are a part of this story."

I grabbed Brenda by the shoulders and stared angrily into her eyes. "If you mention my name in your article—or my initials—or hint at my description—I will never speak to you again, Brenda Tuna."

"Well, if you insist," said Brenda.

"I insist."

Brenda spent the entire weekend writing. I spent it recovering the use of my arms and resting. On Monday she handed her copy to Lawrence. On Thursday the *Crier* was distributed to homerooms. The staff had approved a quarter-page headline that read POPULARITY BREEDS CONTEMPT—FOR YOU. The subheadline said Lunchtime Tapes Reveal Shocking Attitudes at Florence Senior High. Lawrence had given Brenda a byline.

I walked with Brenda to our first class, which was English with Osgood the Terrible.

"Look at them, India, they're actually reading the *Crier* while they're walking." Students were bumping into each other as they made their way to their classes. Some of them were laughing. Others were scowling, and others looked surprised.

"Whoopee," I said without enthusiasm.

"What's your problem, India? Aren't you happy for me on my first day of journalistic fame?"

"I'm worried."

"No reason to be."

Mr. Osgood had his copy of the *Florence Weekly Crier* neatly folded on his desk.

"Nasty little piece of yellow journalism, Tunafish," he said. A few kids laughed nervously. Brenda smiled at him and took her seat.

"It's no such thing," she answered.

"Then why don't you explain to the class exactly what you

had in mind when you wrote this."

"Awareness. Equality. The danger of creating a miniroyalty in a school, the end of all cliques . . ." Brenda would have gone on but Osgood interrupted her.

"Enough. Sounds like commie propaganda to me. Take out your assignments."

During the walk to our second-period classes, I noticed that a number of kids were arguing with each other. A few pointed to Brenda and looked hostile. Brenda was too proud of herself to notice.

"Uh-oh," I said.

"What?" she asked.

"They're getting upset about the article."

"Why? I didn't mention names. I didn't accuse anyone of anything. I simply reported what the *popular* kids say about the rest of us every day. I talked about individualism and pride. It was a very uplifting piece of writing. See you after fourth period."

Brenda and I had different third and fourth period classes. Without her presence, kids talked freely about what they had read. Nobody seemed interested in Brenda's theories. Everyone was quoting from the verbatim transcripts of the lunchtime tapes. They were trying to figure out who had said what about whom.

"Nobody cares about your theories, Brenda." We were eating lunch. We had a table to ourselves. Nobody seemed to want to sit near Brenda. "They probably think you're going to bug their milk cartons."

"It might take time for my ideas to sink in. You'll see, India, by next week, there won't be a clique left in this school. Not a single adolescent will waste a second of life wishing to be a *popular* kid, because the popular kids have been exposed for being what they are."

"Can it, Brenda. I read the article. Look around you. You're in trouble. You shattered their illusions. They wanted to believe in what you called the Great Delusion. They wanted to believe that one day they would wake up, look in the mirror, and find they had become pimpleless, fat-free, small-nosed beauties or muscled, fine-featured strong men—members of the *popular* group."

"An empty goal. I proved that in my article. I showed them that they are regarded as nerds and jerks and less than human by the very people they idolize."

"Their feelings are hurt. Their dreams are shattered. They are angry at you. So are at least the fifteen or so hard-core popular girls we tape-recorded. So are their athletic boyfriends. The article embarrassed them. It may have jeopardized their status. We shall soon be pounded into pulp."

"Not you, India. I left your name out of it."

"Don't forget who sat at the other table for a week. I can be identified." I didn't look anyone in the eye for the rest of the day.

▽ ▽ ▽

THE last bell rang. As the students left school, they demonstrated their anger by shredding the *Crier* and tossing the pieces in the air. I grabbed Brenda by the arm.

"Girls' room," I ordered, and dragged her through a door. We hid out for a half hour and then headed for the newspaper office. The working staff was sitting around looking pleased.

"A great success, Scoop," said Lawrence.

"Don't call me Scoop."

"Why? It's a great compliment for a reporter to be called Scoop," said Lawrence.

"Not if your last name is Tuna."

Everyone began laughing. "Will Ace be acceptable to you?"

"Brenda Tuna, ace reporter, sounds just fine to me."

"Hey," I interrupted. "The entire school is covered with shredded newspapers, Brenda and I had to hide out in the girls' room, and at least three-quarters of the school would like to string Brenda up. How can all of you be so happy?"

"Everyone actually read the paper today."

"And reacted."

"And talked about what they'd read."

"It was great!" The entire staff was chattering away.

"But they didn't really understand what the article was about!" I shouted over the din.

"Some of them did," said Lawrence.

"All they cared about was the gossip on the tapes," I complained.

"They'll draw their own conclusions when they think about it," said a smug Brenda.

"No, they'll simply forget about the article because they don't like its content. I give them about three days. Why don't you stay home tomorrow, Brenda. Everything should be cool by Monday." Lawrence sounded sure of himself.

"Impossible," said Brenda.

"No, a fact of teenage life. It will all be wiped from the consciousness of the school by Monday. Right, staff?"

The staff agreed with Lawrence. Brenda stayed home on Friday. By Monday the only people who seemed to remember Brenda's investigative debut were the members of the custodial staff. We were in the *Crier* office planning the next issue.

"I can't believe that kids in this town are limited by a three-day memory span," said Brenda.

"Only when they want to be. They are choosing not to remember your article, Brenda."

"Let's get on with this paper," said Lawrence. "Any ideas for another superissue?"

"As a matter of fact," said Brenda, "I have been thinking of one terrific subject."

"We're going to be billed the next time the student body shreds the *Crier* all over the school," said Charles, the club treasurer, "and we can't afford it."

"Don't worry, this will be an issue the students will keep forever," said Brenda.

▽ ▽ ▽

TEN

"FINALLY," sighed Brenda. "The second *superissue* of the *Crier* is ready to be put to bed."

"You really love newspaper lingo, don't you, Ace?" said Lawrence.

"I like to use appropriate, colorful language."

"She's right, however she says it. We finished the project and are finally ready to send this issue to the presses," said Ben.

"Finally and maybe final," I said.

"Why are you being so negative, India?" asked Lawrence.

"I'm not being negative. I just learn from experience. I've known Brenda for years. You've only known her for two months. Brenda is my best friend. I would stand back-to-back with her in any battle. She is brilliant, creative, articulate, brave, and original . . ."

"Thank you for your support, India," interrupted Brenda.

"I haven't finished, Brenda. I was going to add . . . and dangerous. I want to go on record as saying that we are playing with fire and we are about to be burned," I finished, and sat down.

"I truly appreciate the fine things India has said about me. Of course I feel obligated to remind you that India has always been a little shy and overcautious," said Brenda. "Besides, it's much too late to do anything else at this point. This issue is ready for publication. We have to meet our deadline."

"Why? This is a school newspaper, not a city daily," said Kether, who had a great deal of common sense.

"Or a town weekly."

"Or a news magazine."

"Or . . ."

"You know perfectly well that all newspapers have to meet deadlines," insisted Brenda, "including the Crier."

"Where is that written, in the Constitution of the United States?" I asked.

"You're just getting nervous about the content of this issue. It's perfectly legitimate journalism based on weeks of good, solid research and careful reporting," said Lawrence.

"Is there some problem here today?" Mrs. Marchar, our club sponsor, leaned into the office. "Aren't you supposed to be on your way to the printer with this week's issue?"

Mrs. Marchar had very little to do with us most of the time. She showed up at the Crier office for approximately two minutes twice a week. No one had ever seen her actually take a single step into Crier space. Mrs. Marchar claimed to believe that students learned best from each other without adult interference.

Each visit, head in our office, feet in the hallway, Mrs.

Marchar would make the following speech: "Don't forget, I'm available for consultation anytime. Just remember, stick to the truth and don't write anything purposely malicious. Any questions? I must run now."

That day, Mrs. Marchar looked worried. We waited for the speech so we could get on with our discussion, but Mrs. Marchar held on to the door frame, cleared her throat, and looked nervous.

"She's not making her speech."

"She looks upset."

Mrs. Marchar had our full attention. A couple of kids cleared their throats. A few people coughed. Finally Mrs. Marchar spoke.

"You haven't written anything you shouldn't have, have you? You are remembering not to libel anyone, aren't you?" Before we could answer, she went on: "The students aren't going to litter the school with shredded *Criers* again, are they? Mr. Bingham, your principal and mine, is still upset about that particular issue. He calls you subversives—says you are trying to undermine the natural social order of high school. He has just reminded me once again that I am responsible for this enterprise. He thinks you're up to something."

"Ridiculous. We've printed perfectly acceptable *Criers* for weeks. Don't you believe in leaving us to our own fate?" said Brenda.

"Philosophically, yes. Technically, I am the club sponsor and in charge of things." Mrs. Marchar was looking at her watch, not us.

"You don't have to worry about a thing," said Lawrence. "We're just having a small disagreement—editorial policy. The *Crier* is ready, and I think we can guarantee that not one single issue will be shredded by a student."

"Well, that's very reassuring. I'd like to stay and chat but I have an appointment." Mrs. Marchar left so fast that she seemed to vanish into thin air.

"She does that very well," said Brenda.

"Better than any stage magician I've ever seen," said Lawrence.

"I was sure she was going to come into the office," said Ben.

"No way," said Lawrence. "She's just worried that Bingham will replace her and she'll lose the extra pay."

"Bingham wouldn't do that, would he? I couldn't work with some adult watching me all the time," said Sue.

"And giving us suggestions . . ."

"And orders . . ."

"What teacher would want to hang around with the bunch of us every day—regardless of money?" said Lawrence.

"Which brings us back to the argument. This issue could be called malicious," I warned.

"No, it can't," said Brenda, "because whatever we are saying is the truth. Our purpose was not to find negative opinions, just opinions."

"Remember that there are going to be some very angry people tomorrow—and we're the available targets," I said.

"Right. How is it going to look on our college applications if we get into trouble?" asked Sue.

"Joining the bimbos, Sue?" asked Lawrence.

Sue turned bright red. "Eat crabgrass, Lawrence. Let's vote. I'll go along with the majority if the vote is secret."

"Eight to two with one abstention," announced Lawrence after counting the ballots. "We go to press."

The next morning the newspapers were delivered to the school by the printer and distributed to the homerooms by us. The headline on the front page got everyone's instant attention.

RATING THE FACULTY
FLORENCE HIGH STUDENTS SPEAK OUT

Even though I was sure the article would lead to our downfall, I have to admit that I was proud of how hard we had worked to gather our information. Every teacher was covered in our survey. We hadn't allowed the survey to become a personality contest. We had concentrated on academic and real classroom issues. It was a solid piece of work.

The math experts on our staff had designed a complicated scoring system. It was impartial, honest, and totally fair. Most of us had spent most of our waking hours for an entire week tabulating the results. Brenda had written the lead article. In it she explained how the survey had been done. Rating the Faculty took up the entire issue. We listened with pride as our fellow students expressed their approval of our hard work. As far as we could tell, the faculty was mildly divided on the issue. The administration hadn't expressed an opinion all day.

"All in all, a successful effort," crowed Brenda.

It was Friday afternoon in the Crier office. We were all feeling pretty good. Even I had begun to relax.

"I can't believe we got away with it," I said.

"Got away with what?" Mr. Bingham's voice bounced off the walls of our small office.

"Hello, Mr. Bingham," said Lawrence. "Welcome to our humble office."

"Cut the bull, Mr. Snyder. I am here to read you delinquents the riot act. From now on this newspaper will be a regular high-school newspaper—standard, temperate, and without controversy. You will confine yourselves to writing articles about school activities—such as dances, plays, and sporting events. You will refrain from expressing your radical opinions about your fellow students, faculty, school policy, or anything else for that matter."

"So much for freedom of the press," grumbled Brenda.

"This is a high school, Miss Tuna. There is no freedom of the press here."

"That's not constitutional," argued Lawrence.

"Hire a lawyer and sue me," said Mr. Bingham. "In the meantime, Mrs. Marchar has been relieved of her sponsorship duties. Until I can find someone to take her place, I will supervise this paper. You will show me everything—*everything*—do you understand?—that is to be printed. I will have final editorial say. Are we in agreement with this new policy?"

"No," said Brenda.

"No," said Lawrence.

"No," said the rest of us.

"WHAT?" shouted a surprised Mr. Bingham.

"No, we do not agree with that new policy. It's unfair. It's censorship. It's muzzling the free press. . . ."

"It's boring," added Ben.

"You have no choice," said Mr. Bingham. "I am the principal."

"It's our club. You can't fire us from a school club," said Brenda.

"But I can assign you to detention until you comply. As of Monday, the staff of the *Weekly Crier* will meet in the guidance office after school."

"For how many days?" asked Sue.

"For as long as it takes," said Mr. Bingham as he left the room.

"Don't say it, India," said Lawrence.

"Say what?" I asked innocently.

"I told you so," he said.

"But I did, didn't I?"

▽ ▽ ▽

WE were in detention for an entire two weeks. We had planned to appeal to the student body for support by publishing an issue of the *Crier* from the detention room, but Mr. Bingham froze our club funds. So Brenda taught us a bunch of protest songs from the 1960s, and we spent our time singing and getting to know the other delinquents. Word of our incarceration got around, and free students began to drop in to offer moral support. Some brought snacks. A couple brought guitars. By the first Friday the detention room was filled to capacity. By the following Monday the crowd overflowed into the hallway. By Wednesday it seemed as if half the school population was opting to stay after school with us.

It was only two days before Christmas break. We added Christmas carols to our repertoire.

"Do you think Bingham will make us do time right up to vacation?" asked Ben.

"I hope so," whispered Fred, the most timid kid I had ever met. Much to everyone's surprise he had spent most of his detention time talking to some tough guy in a leather jacket.

"I'm never giving in," said Brenda. Someone began strumming chords on a guitar.

"Before you begin another round of sour notes"—a shiver

went down my spine—"you had better listen to the good news."
Mr. Osgood, Teacher of English, torturer of students, and re-
cipient of the lowest faculty score in our survey, pushed students
aside as he made his way into the detention room.

"Good news from you, Mr. Osgood?" asked Brenda sweetly.

"From me and for me, Tunafish. The staff members of the
former *Weekly Crier* are dismissed from detention."

"A general amnesty?" asked Sue.

"What do you mean by former *Weekly Crier?*" asked Brenda.

"Your little radical club has been disbanded by the administration. I have been appointed sponsor of the *New Weekly Crier.*
Your former club funds are our funds now. I shall choose a suitable
writing staff after vacation. If any of you are interested in joining
me in this new enterprise, you may apply for club membership
at that time." Osgood laughed an evil laugh and continued:

"You may now leave, baby reporters. Pick up your personal
belongings from the newspaper office immediately. I have had
the lock changed and will turn the key in exactly thirty minutes.
If you are inside when that happens, you will starve to death
during the Christmas break. Anything left behind that is not
school property will be disposed of in the evening trash." Osgood
left the room humming.

"What a creep!"

"I wouldn't join a club sponsored by him for a million
dollars."

"Yes, you would."

"I'm depressed."

"I'm angry."

"My coat's in the office."

The detention room emptied. Word spread through the
crowd in the hall, and students began leaving the school.

"Like rats deserting a sinking ship," mumbled someone.

The staff of the former *Weekly Crier* and a few of the friendlier delinquents moved quickly toward our former office.

▽ ▽ ▽

ELEVEN

EVEN though some of the kids were crying and all of us were completely demoralized, Brenda didn't miss a beat.

"Cheer up, staff. Let's get our stuff out of here so we can begin phase two of our newspaper careers," she announced as she tossed her personal belongings into a cardboard carton.

"I always knew the woman was mad." Lawrence spoke to no one in particular. He was sulking in a corner.

"Didn't you hear the crud?" asked Ben. "We're banned from the *Crier*."

"Maybe Brenda has jobs lined up for us on the *New York Times*."

"Or the *Washington Post*."

"Brenda is just suffering from shock," I said, defending my cheerful friend, who was whistling and smiling to herself. I suspected that she had gone completely off the deep end.

"I feel like giving this school a shock."

"Yeah, I'm really angry. Let's trash this office."

"No, let's sit in," suggested a more level head.

"Look where our last sit-in got us."

"That wasn't a sit-in. We were in detention."

"You're right, man. It's time for real action." One of the detention regulars was smashing his fist into the palm of his hand over and over.

"Who are you?" Brenda had come out of her trance and was staring at the leather-jacketed delinquent.

64

"He's my friend Slick," whispered little Fred. "He was in detention with us the entire time. Slick is a loyal supporter of our cause and a very interesting person."

"I'll bet he is," said Brenda, staring Slick in the eye. Slick winked at Brenda. Brenda turned quickly toward the rest of us.

"Have any of you ever heard of underground newspapers?"

"Sure," said Slick. Brenda ignored him.

"Well?" she demanded.

"You mean smut?"

"No, not smut. Underground newspapers—papers that are printed outside of the established publishing channels."

"Illegally?"

"No, not illegally, nor illicitly, nor immorally." Brenda was getting impatient. She kept looking at her watch.

"Then what, Brenda?"

"Just outside of the establishment. We create a newspaper by ourselves. We set up a free press. We write whatever we want and distribute it to the students—outside of school where nobody can stop us."

"Oh."

"Wow."

"Can we afford to do that?" asked Charles, the former *Crier* treasurer.

"We can't let lack of money stop us."

"Right."

"Let's do it."

Smiles were beginning to appear on staff faces. I had to hand it to Brenda, she seemed to be pulling us out of a mess.

"I'll help out. I have a rod. I'll distribute the papers for you." Slick, the fist-smasher, had spoken.

"A rod? You have a gun?" Fred's voice squeaked with nervousness.

"Not a gun, pimple face. A hot rod, wheels, man." He slapped Fred on the back in a friendly gesture. Fred grabbed the wall to keep from falling over.

"Thanks, Slick. If you and any of your friends want to help, we'll be grateful." Brenda nodded in the direction of the small bunch of detention regulars surrounding Slick.

"No sweat, cute stuff."

"If you ever call me cute stuff again, I'll take your face off, Slick."

"No sweat, Brenda."

By this time Brenda was hopping from foot to foot with impatience. "Do you have everything that is ours? Then let's get out of here. You're all invited to my house for a meeting."

"What's going on here? We heard you had been expelled and the newspaper was closed down. What are we going to do about our credits for college?" The six bimbos had arrived.

"Buzz off, bimbos," said Lawrence. "The *New Florence Weekly Crier* is all yours. Your sponsor will be arriving momentarily."

We eased the bimbos aside and began leaving the *Crier* office for the last time. We could hear Osgood jingling his keys as we moved toward the nearest exit, loaded down with every book, pencil, scrap of paper, and staple that had not been bought with school funds. Osgood arrived at the office door as Brenda nudged the last of us into the hallway.

"Merry Christmas, Mr. Osgood," said Brenda cheerfully as she brushed past him.

"Happy New Year," the rest of us added.

"What are you up to?" Mr. Osgood called after us as we marched out of the building singing "The Battle Hymn of the Republic."

That afternoon, the *Florence Free Press* was born. Slick joined our staff as distribution manager—two of his leather-jacketed friends volunteered to be his personal crew. Slick introduced them as "My men, The Boys."

"I suppose you have real names," said Brenda.

Slick and The Boys stared at her but didn't respond. Brenda sighed loudly, shrugged her shoulders, and dropped the subject.

Mrs. Tuna invited the fourteen rebel newspaper persons to stay for dinner and managed to feed all of us until we couldn't move. She took a special liking to Slick, who not only ate the homemade goat cheese in his salad—but the goat cheese most everyone else tried to politely hide in their napkins or under the edges of their plates.

"I love this stuff, Mrs. T. You are some great cook." Mrs. Tuna beamed as Slick wiped his mouth on his bare arm.

"Let's get back to business, staff." Brenda had a big yellow pad in front of her. "We need an operating budget. Any ideas?"

"Sell advertising."

"How can we sell advertising for a paper that doesn't exist yet?" Charles had always been the practical member of our organization.

"Have a garage sale."

"Have a bake sale."

"Ask our parents."

The bad ideas came fast and furiously. Then a voice boomed out, "Everyone chip in."

"Chip in?"

"Yeah, chip in," Slick said. "Put your money where your mouths are. Chip in. You all get allowances." Slick was sprawled on the floor leaning back on his elbows. An unlit cigarette hung from his mouth.

Brenda looked at Slick almost as if she liked him.

"He's right. It's the best idea so far. Let's figure out how much allowance we each get a month." Brenda began writing.

"Our whole allowance? Come on, Brenda, give us a break. I need walking-around money."

"Right, Brenda, that's asking too much."

"Stop whining. Nobody wants your whole allowance. But even if we did, a little personal sacrifice is good for the spirit. Do you all agree to this plan?" Even The Boys voted yes.

It turned out that we could each afford to give ten dollars a month—with some sacrificing. That gave us a monthly budget of one hundred forty dollars—not nearly enough to have the *Florence Free Press* printed professionally.

"There's an old offset machine in my uncle's garage," Slick said. "Let's liberate it."

"Steal? You want us to steal something?" One of the more timid kids was beginning to panic.

"Not steal, liberate. He hasn't used it in years. It's obsolete."

"Does it work?" asked Charles.

"Sure, I used to use it when I was a kid. You type or draw on stencils, ink up the machine, turn it on, and it prints like a bandit."

"Doesn't your uncle need it anymore?"

"With computers and instant printing stores, he says it's too much trouble."

"What did he use it for, Slick?" Brenda asked.

"Pamphlets. Flyers. Different stuff."

"What kind of pamphlets?" One of the former copyboys was practicing being an investigative interviewer.

"Look, pip-squeak, back off. Do you want the machine or not?"

"Was it pornography? Was he printing radical political stuff? Maybe your uncle is a counterfeiter? Was he printing money on the press?" The fledgling reporter was on his feet, scribbling notes on a small pad while he headed toward Slick.

"I'm going to stuff your foot in your mouth unless you back off and shut up, mushbrain," warned Slick.

"We want the press," said Brenda, ignoring the interruption and possibly saving the kid's life.

"Shouldn't we vote?" someone asked.

"If the boss lady wants the machine, it's hers," said Slick.

Brenda smiled sweetly at Slick and called for a vote. The heavy, dusty offset machine appeared on Brenda's driveway the next morning, along with boxes of stencils and a number of cans of black ink. Brenda woke up to find Slick and The Boys drinking coffee and eating whole wheat cereal with her mother in the kitchen.

Slick, Brenda, and The Boys spent hours cleaning the machine. By the time I arrived at noon, they had managed to move it to the Tuna basement and were inking the rollers and inserting paper into the holding tray. I watched as they printed up twenty copies of a very funny caricature of Mr. Osgood.

"Let's not waste paper," said Slick, turning off the machine.

"This is really good," I said. "Who drew it?" I knew it couldn't have been Brenda.

"Slick did."

"Slick did?" I sounded stupidly surprised and was immediately sorry.

"Yeah, I took a few minutes off from robbing stores and mugging old people."

"I'm sorry, Slick." I really was.

"Sure. When do we get to work, Brenda?"

"Immediately. Let's call a meeting."

TWELVE

IT was a great half year for the staff of the *Florence Free Press*. We produced a newspaper about every three weeks. Slick and The Boys made sure every one of the fifteen hundred copies of each issue was put into the actual hands of a student, a teacher, or an ordinary local citizen. We had one hundred percent distribution.

By the third issue we were printing a professional-looking newspaper that included cartoons, a gossip column, a consumer column, and feature articles. We paid close attention to everything we wrote, but for some the most important part of each issue was what Brenda called "our investigative coups"—our headline stories.

The first coup was a medical exposé—of sorts—The Athlete's Foot Scandal. Our investigative staff solved the mystery of the ongoing student foot rot epidemic at the high school. It was a small scandal as scandals go, but putting it in print prevented a whole lot of kids from having their feet disintegrate during adolescence. We weren't exactly considered heroes, but the kids at school began to view the *Florence Free Press* as a good source of information.

After that we launched our disappearing bird series. Actually, it wasn't meant to be a series; it's just that two interesting stories of missing birds in Florence occurred around the same time.

The first was about geese on Moon Pond. They had lived there for years—winter and summer—and now they were gone. It was one of The Boys who noticed that Moon Pond had a very strange smell—like spoiled milk. We traced the smell up a stream and discovered a hobbyist who was making cheese in his basement and pouring the leftover liquid into the rushing water. He thought the waste liquid was organic and harmless. A week after he stopped dumping it, Moon Pond smelled like a pond again and one pair of geese had begun building a nest.

The second bird story was uncovered a few weeks later and was a little weirder. It involved missing pigeons. Where there had once been at least fifty pigeons using the statue of Thaddeus Thaddeus in the village green as a roost and toilet, there were now two. What we discovered made a number of people a little sick and very angry. Florence had been struck by a pigeon-poaching ring that trapped wild park pigeons and sold them to fancy restaurants as prime squab.

"What does it matter? A squab *is* a pigeon."

"These were park pigeons. They weren't meant to be eaten."

"Who's to say what birds are meant to be eaten? You eat chicken, don't you?"

"That's different."

"Why?"

"Because these were wild birds. Would you eat a robin or a blue jay?"

"If I was starving, I guess."

"Let's just get this issue to press."

"We're in a rut," I complained one afternoon. We had distributed our fifth issue and were having our weekly staff meeting at Pierre's Continental Pizza. Everyone was beginning to look bored—except Brenda.

"No more bird stories, please."

"One was really a pollution story."

"It had birds in it."

"We should write something about the school."

"We always have articles about the school."

"Not headline articles. We need something big. Something for the front page," I said.

"Funny you should mention that, India," said Brenda. "It just so happens that Coleman found something interesting at school this week." Brenda sat back and waited for this news to sink in. We were silent for a few moments.

"What?"

"Coleman?"

"Coleman?"

"*Our* Coleman?" Coleman's nickname was "The Invisible Man." He was an intensely shy, pale, short, thin, quiet kid who had never asked to be a reporter. Mostly he made himself useful in small essential ways. We all liked Coleman, but no one had ever heard him say more than three words consecutively.

"Tell them, Coleman," Brenda encouraged.

Coleman cleared his throat twice and stared at his un-touched slice of pizza. He was blushing.

"Go on, Coleman. We all want to hear."

"Right, Coleman. Speak."

The more we encouraged him, the darker red he became.

"Coleman, if you don't talk this minute, I'm going to twist your nose off your face." Slick leaned over and grabbed Coleman's nose.

Everyone started getting furious at Slick—except Coleman. He began to laugh. So did Slick. Slick ruffled Coleman's hair. Coleman spoke.

"I found a room."

"What kind of room, Coleman?"

"Shut up and let the kid talk," ordered Slick.

"A kind of storeroom. At school. It has stuff in it that shouldn't be there. It was unlocked so I went in. Well, it wasn't really unlocked."

"You broke in? You, Coleman?"

"Not exactly. I'm good at opening locks. It was easy."

"Good man, Coleman," said Slick.

"What did you find, Coleman?" about six kids asked.

"Maybe you had better finish eating your pizza first," said Coleman as he shoved his aside. That was when I noticed that Brenda hadn't eaten her pizza, either.

"I won't talk here," said Coleman. "It's too public."

"Will my house do?" asked Brenda.

Coleman nodded. We left the pizza parlor in silence and hurried through the darkening streets. We could feel something important was about to happen. What we never guessed was that our most nauseating news story was about to break.

▽ ▽ ▽

THIRTEEN

NEWSPAPER people are sometimes very much like spies. They are suspicious, cautious, and secretive. We didn't say another word about Coleman's discovery until we got behind the tall fence of the Luna house.

"Okay, Coleman, talk."

"Right. What's this all about?"

"What were you doing snooping around school storerooms?"

"Tell us," demanded the staff.

In the dark of the sheep meadow, Coleman seemed to lose his inability to speak.

73

"Since September I've felt that the school lunches were terrible, . . ." he began.

"So what else is new?"

"Big deal."

"You should be a food critic."

Coleman ignored the sarcasm and continued. "Much worse than last year. In addition to bad cooking, I began to suspect that the quality of the food being used was inferior."

"Yawn," said someone.

"This is what you consider a story?"

"This is worse than more birds."

"The next person who interrupts the kid gets ground into dust," warned Slick.

"Thank you," said Coleman. "I looked up the school budget and found that our district spends more per student on lunch food than any other school on Long Island. Technically, we should be receiving gourmet-quality meals."

"Come on, Coleman. Be real."

"Right. We have a school cafeteria, not a restaurant."

Slick growled. The voices in the dark were quiet.

"So, I knew that something was very wrong and I decided to explore the school kitchen. I found some interesting evidence. The shelves in the storerooms were filled with bags of government surplus flour, cans of lard, boxes of powdered eggs, and stacks of no-brand cans of vegetables, juices, bottles of ketchup, mayonnaise, et cetera."

"Never heard of Etcetera. Is it some kind of bean?"

"No, it's a kind of noodle."

"That's it, bozos," said Slick.

"Please don't hurt them, Slick," said Coleman politely. "I'll get to the point."

Coleman took a breath and went on speaking. "Everything in the school kitchen and storerooms was of the cheapest quality. So where was the food money being spent? The storerooms had been pretty easy to enter with my master key, but the big refrigerated room was locked with a monstrous padlock."

"You have a master key?"

"Locks are my hobby," said Coleman. We could hear Slick and The Boys chuckling in the darkness.

"So you used the master key on the padlock, right?"

"Wrong. Padlocks have different key sizes from door locks. Haven't you ever noticed that? I had to pick the padlock."

"But that was breaking and entering. You broke the law," someone said nervously.

"Technically, I broke the law when I used my illegal master key to get into the storerooms. But I wasn't going to steal anything. I was investigating a news story."

"What news story?"

"Stop interrupting him," I demanded, "and use your heads. Think about what Coleman is telling us."

"What?"

"Right."

"I think I understand."

"I don't."

"What are you all talking about?"

Our staff was at very different levels of intellectual sophistication.

"What was in the refrigerated storeroom, Coleman?" asked Slick.

"Well, actually, it was a freezer—a very large, walk-in freezer," said Coleman.

"And what was in it?"

There was silence.

"Coleman?"

"Coleman?"

"Did he leave?"

"Did he faint or something? He is a nervous kid."

"No, I can see his shadow. He just got up. He's standing behind me."

"Coleman, tell them," said Brenda.

Coleman's voice had gotten very soft and angry-sounding. "Ice cream, frozen pizzas, and . . ."

"And . . . ?" we all asked.

"And meat. Lots and lots of stacks of boxes of meat—mostly in the form of hamburger patties."

"So?" someone asked.

"That's it? This is stupid."

"Tell them, Coleman," demanded Brenda.

Coleman mumbled something.

"We couldn't hear you."

"It was HORSEMEAT!" shouted Coleman.

"Oh."

"Oh, no."

"That's disgusting."

"I think I'm going to be sick."

"I *am* getting sick."

"Do you know how many burgers I've eaten in that cafeteria in the past three years?"

"I'll never eat meat again."

"I'll never eat anything again."

"I'll never be able to look a horse in the eye again."

"Oh."

Then, except for a whole lot of groaning, there was silence.

I understood why Brenda and Coleman couldn't eat their pizza during the meeting.

"We have to do something about it." Coleman spoke in a sick-sounding voice. "Someone is ripping off the kids and buying cheap food instead of what they're supposed to buy."

"Is horsemeat cheap?" asked one of The Boys, gagging.

"Costs a whole lot less than beef."

"I ate horseburgers."

"I ate a relative of Black Beauty." One of the girls was crying.

"Stop this!" shouted Brenda. "We're all sick about the meat we've eaten in the cafeteria and we all feel terrible, but . . ."

"I don't," said Eric, the consumer columnist.

"You don't?" People began moving away from him.

"Horse is just another hoofed animal. Besides, equine meat is less fatty than beef—better for you."

"You're disgusting."

"I am not. Horsemeat is a very popular protein source in some European countries."

"You're gross."

"You're a barbarian."

"You're a cannibal."

"Hah! I'd only be a cannibal if I ate people. Any people in the freezer, Coleman?"

The Boys jumped Eric and began pummeling him.

"Cut it out!" ordered Brenda. The Boys continued to pound on Eric.

"Do something, Slick, please," Brenda pleaded.

"Cease and desist!" Slick demanded. The Boys sat down—on Eric.

"I can't breathe," he gasped.

"Away," said Slick in a quiet, tight voice. Eric was spared.

"Now let's get organized. This isn't just about eating horses. It's a story about fraud. We are going to blast this scandal into the open, but our timing has to be perfect," said Brenda.

"We'll need school lunchroom budget figures," said Charles.

"And the names of the people who do the ordering," I added.

"And the names of the people who sign for deliveries."

"Who in the kitchen knows exactly what they are using for ingredients?"

"Who in the kitchen doesn't know?"

"How long has this been going on?"

Despite the shock and horror most of us were feeling, we were functioning like the incredible investigative team we had become. We were newspaper people.

We decided that because of the nature of the story, we would get our next issue out fast. The last thing we wanted was to be accused by our fellow students of keeping this information from them.

"Three days. Can we do it in three days so everyone can read it by Friday morning—before lunch?" asked Slick.

"If we do a special issue—an Extra with nothing in it but this article," said Brenda.

We all agreed, divided up assignments, and began to leave.

"Just remember," Brenda called after us, "don't eat the hamburgers in the cafeteria this week."

"Or the meatballs," added someone.

"Or the spaghetti meat sauce."

"Or the meat loaf."

"Or the chili."

"Or the stew."

"Who eats the stew?"

"Do you think the hot dogs are safe?"

"I'm going to bring my lunch."

"I'm going to eat salad."

"I agree with Eric. I can't see anything wrong with horse-meat. I'm sticking with my regular lunch. Why don't you do a consumer report on the merits of eating horse versus the merits of eating cow, Eric?"

"I'm going to throw up."

▽ ▽ ▽

FOURTEEN

IT wasn't easy, but by Friday morning we had the Extra edition of the *Florence Free Press* written, printed, and stashed in our school lockers. This was something of a miracle, because as of late Thursday evening, we had still been arguing with each other.

"Our efforts have not been without a certain amount of disagreement about newspaper policy. Fortunately, we are finally in agreement." Brenda had never sounded happier.

The staff of the *Florence Free Press* was in the Tuna living room collating newspapers and tying them in bundles.

"Says who? The Extra looks just like an issue of the *National Enquirer*," complained Charles.

"The headline will get the reader's attention," said Brenda.

"That's the excuse used by every muckraking rag," said Lawrence, chuckling.

"What's so funny?" asked Charles. "Are you happy to be associated with a low-grade production?"

"It's not low-grade. We have not written a story about a three-headed, green baby from Venus. Our article is about an important, real matter," Brenda insisted.

"And what about the headline?" I asked. I read it aloud: "BLACK BEAUTY BURGERS SERVED TO STUDENTS!"

We had had a number of fights about the headline, which took up the entire front page. The sensationalists, led by Brenda, won by one vote.

"What's wrong with that headline?" asked Brenda, innocently.

"It's an exaggeration. It's untrue. It does not say anything about misuse of funds. It's inflammatory. It's emotional. It will make the students crazy. I don't understand how you of all people can support such rot, Brenda. You've always talked about truth and justice. . . ."

Brenda interrupted me. "It's not untrue. Not really. It's symbolic. In any case, it's highly effective."

"It will cause a riot," I said.

"Not in Florence," said Brenda.

In a way we were both right. Slick and The Boys cut school Friday morning and delivered copies of the Extra to members of the school board, the chief of police, the mayor, the cable television news anchor, the local newspapers, the nearest office of the regional newspaper, and the president of the PTA. The rest of us began passing out copies to students, teachers, and administrators at the beginning of the first lunch period.

The reaction of students to the Extra depended upon two things—individual attitudes about eating horsemeat and whether or not a student had taken a bite out of a school hamburger just before reading the article. There was a fair amount of lamenting, screaming, crying, outrage, arguing, and loud, bad jokes. The cafeteria emptied. A number of students stood around outside the school looking green. Others heatedly discussed the fraud aspect of the story, and many took the opportunity to lounge in the sun. Vegetarians walked through the crowd instilling guilt in meat-eaters. Meat-eaters swore they would only eat chicken in the future. Eric, who apparently had little conscience, recruited a small group of adventurous students and formed the Continental Cuisine Eating Club. He and his band of hungry experimenters sauntered into the school to sample and judge the horsemeat fare.

Nobody trashed the cafeteria. No fist fights broke out. The several hundred students in front of the school were peacefully upset. It was a typical Florence scene. There seemed to be more dramatics than real passion. Then Mr. Bingham appeared on the steps. He held his arms above his head and shouted for our attention. A copy of the Extra was clutched in one hand.

"This is a pack of untruths," he yelled, waving the paper in the air. "Calm down. Go inside. Return to the cafeteria. Midday gatherings on the school front lawn are forbidden. Return to the building now and you won't be punished." It was the wrong thing for him to say. The mildly agitated crowd began to turn into a mob.

"*Punished?* You've been feeding us *slop* instead of food!"

"You made us eat horsemeat."

"I don't even feed my *dog* horsemeat."

The students had all turned to face Mr. Bingham. They did not look friendly. Mr. Bingham tried to respond. "We'll look into this matter. Just calm down . . ."

Before he could go any further, the bell rang. The second lunch period had begun. I think that if Bingham hadn't been standing on the steps waving his arms, most of the kids would have gone to their classrooms. But there he stood, a symbol of the adult world—authority, superiority, power, cafeteria food, horsemeat—blocking the way. Nobody moved toward the school. In a few minutes, hundreds of students from the second lunch period were pushing past Mr. Bingham to join their now-famished classmates on the lawn. Each had a copy of the Extra. Some were actually reading the article.

"Ahhhh." Brenda sighed. She threw her arm around my shoulder and said, "I told you there wouldn't be a riot."

At that moment a mass of students surged toward the front doors. Mr. Bingham was swept back into the school with the ravenous mob.

"Where are you going?" someone shouted.

"We're storming the cafeteria," a kid called over his shoulder.

"Bring me a cheese sandwich. I'll pay you," cried a desperate voice to no one in particular.

In a remarkably short time, the students were outside once more. They had bought every salad, yogurt, container of milk, slice of bread, morsel of cheese, and dessert available.

A fleet-footed senior with a pocketful of money had been at the head of the line. He set up a concession on the steps, doubled the price of everything, and completely sold out his stock in ten minutes. Kids who had brought lunch from home were treated like royalty until their brown paper bags were empty and crumpled on the ground.

"This is not a pretty sight, Brenda," I said.

Before she could answer, the public-address system crackled on.

"Pzzzzst. Arrrgh. Go pzzzzgrt zzt your klzzzz."

"Anyone understand that?"

"What?"

"The announcement."

"What announcement?"

The P.A. system screeched as someone tried to adjust the volume. Hands flew to ears. The loudspeakers screamed. Then, over the complaining shouts of the hundreds of kids and the horrible noise of the public-address system, we heard sirens. Everyone turned toward the street.

Two squad cars, the mayor's limousine, a car from the health department, the local cable news truck, and a bunch of private cars were pulling up in front of the school. Adults of all sizes and shapes slammed out of the cars and marched toward the school building, shoving students aside as they moved. Many were holding copies of the Extra issue. A few had them rolled tightly in their hands—like small clubs.

"Hey, it's the press."

"It's the police."

"We're going to be on television."

"That's the guy from the pound—you don't think . . ."

"Don't say it."

"That's my mom. Hi, Mom."

The adults ignored the students as they headed for what we supposed was a showdown with the school administration. As they reached the front door, the third lunch-period bell rang and more kids swarmed out of the building. Mr. Bingham appeared on the steps flanked by two policemen and the mayor. Bingham was carrying a bullhorn in one hand and a copy of the infamous Extra in the other. Some of the kids were chanting, "NO MORE HORSEMEAT. NO MORE HORSEMEAT." Others began to shout, "FEED US. FEED US."

"A genuine protest," shouted a proud Brenda.

"Or something. It's about to turn ugly, Brenda. Let's get out of here."

"And miss this journalistic opportunity? Never."

"QUIET!" Mr. Bingham shouted through the bullhorn.

A few kids quieted down.

"QUIET!" he bellowed again. "THESE LADIES AND GENTLEMEN ARE HERE TO HELP KEEP ORDER. WE ARE INVESTIGATING THE RUMORS SPREAD BY THIS FILTHY PIECE OF YELLOW JOURNALISM. . . ." Mr. Bingham shook his copy of the Extra. "THE TRUTH WILL WIN OUT. NOW GO BACK TO YOUR CLASSES AND FINISH THE DAY."

"I smell a cover-up coming," said Brenda.

"They're going to expel us and tell everyone we were lying," moaned Charles.

"Maybe not. Look!" I had spotted Slick and The Boys rounding the corner of the building dragging a metal garbage can and a huge box. They bounced the can up the steps, making as much noise as possible. The police stepped between them and Mr. Bingham.

"We have something for you, Bingham, from the school kitchen." Slick turned to the crowd and held the empty carton with its large, legible label—PRIME HORSEMEAT BURGERS—over his head while The Boys opened the garbage can and started tossing smaller boxes and wrapping paper to waiting hands.

"It says 'Horsemeat burger, one-quarter pound.'"

"This box says 'Stewing meat—ten pounds of horse flank.'"

"Oh, no, it's really true."

The mayor was red in the face and talking very fast into Bingham's ear. The kids, with actual evidence in their hands, and very little protein in their stomachs, were on the edge of hysteria. The Continental Cuisine Eating Club chose that moment to emerge from their horsemeat feast.

"I just want to say," announced Eric to the momentarily

quiet crowd, "that in our opinion, horsemeat is equal to beef. As a matter of fact, it even surpasses . . ."

That was the last straw. The crowd roared and began pelting Eric and the Continental Cuisine Eating Club with the cartons and papers Slick had just distributed. When they ran out of that ammunition, they threw crumpled lunch bags, cellophane wrap, empty milk cartons, and apple cores.

Eric and the other club members ducked behind the pillars, which just happened to be behind Mr. Bingham and the mayor. Missiles followed the direction of their retreat.

"Oh, no," moaned Brenda as a banana skin landed on Mr. Bingham's head.

"It's a good thing kids were so hungry or this entire riot would be a whole lot messier," I said.

"It's not a riot. It's a demonstration," said Brenda.

When the ammunition ran out, the crowd calmed down. Mr. Bingham put the bullhorn to his mouth.

"I'VE DECIDED TO SEND YOU HOME EARLY TO-DAY. SCHOOL BUSES WILL BE READY TO TRANSPORT YOU IN TEN MINUTES. WALKERS LEAVE NOW. THERE WILL BE AN ASSEMBLY FOR THE ENTIRE SCHOOL ON MONDAY AT EIGHT-THIRTY A.M. IN THE GYMNASIUM."

Mr. Bingham turned on his heel and practically ran back into the school. The mayor, the policemen, and the reporters were right behind him.

"We should send in a reporter to cover what's happening," said Brenda.

"Are you kidding?" said Charles.

"Let's just get out of here before they find a way to make us into student burgers," said Lawrence.

85

"It was just a thought," said Brenda.

It was the first weekend since the birth of the *Florence Free Press* that the staff did not rack its brains for newsworthy ideas. Eric wrote a consumer column about horsemeat and a restaurant review of the cafeteria. Nobody would read either piece. We spent our time catching up on homework and wondering what would happen next.

▽ ▽ ▽

FIFTEEN

BY eight-twenty-nine Monday morning, the entire population of Florence Senior High School was crammed into the gym. Students, faculty, maintenance staff, cafeteria personnel, and administrators filled the bleachers, the available floor space, and the doorways. As the minute hand of the gym clock landed on the six, Mr. Bingham, accompanied by the mayor, the president of the school board, and the police chief, walked to the microphone that had been set up for the occasion.

"Our fate is about to be sealed," I whispered to Brenda.

Brenda didn't have a chance to make a snappy reply. Mr. Bingham tapped the microphone and cleared his throat. He looked uncomfortable as he explained to the audience that there had, indeed, been an unfortunate situation concerning the school cafeteria, which involved the purchasing of food and personal profits. It was now cleared up. Arrests had taken place and additional staff were being recruited. He regretted that the problem had been made public by a bunch of disgruntled student misfits and said that Florence would now have to live down the disgrace of the bad publicity that, unfortunately, had become national.

I glanced around and saw that many of the students were smiling. The horsemeat scandal and the student demonstration had gotten a mention on the network evening news on Saturday.

"I wonder if we'll make *People* magazine," I heard someone whisper.

Bingham gave us his personal guarantee that, in the future, the cafeteria would serve first-class, high-quality meals—as had always been the intention of the administration and school board. Bingham went on to say that the kitchen had been partly re-stocked and the freezer full of frozen horsemeat was going to be emptied that very afternoon. A few teachers applauded politely. The students were silent. Then . . .

"They should be buried." Brenda's foggy voice rang out in the quiet gym.

Bingham looked confused. The police chief stepped forward and took the microphone. "We know that you children feel strongly about what the alleged miscreants did, but we have a system of law in this country. If found guilty in a courtroom, they'll pay the penalty . . ."

"Not the crooks. The poor horses. We should bury *them*!" Brenda's voice was clear as a bell.

"What are you doing, Brenda?" I whispered. Brenda el-bowed me in the ribs. Kids around us were giggling.

Mr. Bingham snatched the microphone from the police chief. "What horses?" he shouted, making the public-address system screech.

"The dead horses in the freezer, that's what horses."

"Right. They deserve a burial," someone else joined in.

"It's the least we can do. Bury them. Let's give them a funeral," another voice added.

"We could have a memorial service."

"How about a tombstone. The school should get them a tombstone like in the old west."

"Yeah." "Right." "FUNERAL." "TOMBSTONE." "MEMORIAL SERVICE." Students were shouting and stamping their feet.

It took about five minutes to restore order.

"This is ridiculous." Mr. Bingham was furious. "That's meat in the freezer, not horses. It's chopped up, cut up, butchered, frozen meat."

Wrong words, Bingham, I thought to myself.

Kids began to gag, moan, and groan. Others began shouting and waving their fists in anger. There was no telling how many were actually upset by Bingham's description and how many were just having fun. The effect was the same.

"BURY THEM. BURY THEM. BURY THEM." The kids were stamping their feet and clapping their hands.

"QUIET! QUIET!" Bingham shouted. The police chief looked disgusted. The mayor looked worried. The president of the school board looked as if she wanted to kill Mr. Bingham.

We were herded out of the gym to our first-period classes. Some kids were crying with genuine emotion. Others were laughing so hard they could hardly walk. All seemed in agreement that there should be a horse funeral. As the day progressed, the feeling got stronger among the students. No matter what their reasons, they all believed that the school owed us something. Amends had to be made.

The student body was backed by the school psychologist, who, in an open letter to the community printed in a local newspaper that very afternoon, stated that we psychologically sensitive adolescents had been traumatized terribly. We felt betrayed. We needed a way to heal our collective emotional wounds. A formalized group activity such as a funeral would be just the thing called for. She asked for community support for the project.

Much to everyone's surprise, she got it. So it came to pass that on Friday, exactly one week after the Extra edition of the *Florence Free Press* revealed the shameful facts to the world, the entire student body held a funeral for "our horses." We put on quite a show. The choir sang hymns. The student body president gave a eulogy. We even had a burial. The industrial arts classes had built a small coffin into which had been placed select cuts of the horsemeat. Local florists contributed wreaths of flowers. The art students spent the week painting a huge mural, which they mounted across the back of the gym. During the ceremonies we were forced to look at paintings of strangely colored horses running and grazing in what the art students claimed was horse heaven.

"That's a bit much," said Charles.

"I think it's neat," said Fred.

"Which horse did you paint, Fred?" I asked.

"The blue one on the hill."

"I rest my case," said Charles.

The ceremonies were over. Four members of the football team stepped forward and lifted the coffin onto their shoulders. The student body followed them out of the school to a corner of the front lawn where two holes had been dug. The coffin was lowered into one, and an evergreen tree was set in the other. One by one students filed by—each tossing a single handful of dirt on top of the coffin or the roots of the tree.

Finally two girls stepped forward and placed an engraved brass plaque on the grave. "Equine Memorial Garden. In memory of our beloved friends, the unsuspecting horses who gave their lives to feed the unsuspecting students. We are eternally sorry."

"I guess it will be set in cement," I said.

"As if anyone would want to steal it," said Slick.

"It would make a great souvenir of the weirdness that is Florence," said Lawrence.

"Let's eat. I'm hungry," said Brenda.

The rite of passage complete, the student body was being treated to an after-funeral picnic on the football field—paid for by the PTA. It was a barbecue. There were hamburgers and hot dogs and sausages. Everyone ate heartily.

On Saturday morning the staff met in the Tuna living room to have the first formal meeting of the *Florence Free Press* since the horsemeat Extra was distributed.

"My father says we made Florence into a national joke."

"What national joke? We were a thirty-second filler on the Saturday night network news a week ago. Who watches news on Saturday night?"

"My mother says that if I keep working on the *Free Press*, I'll never get into a decent college."

"My father says that no kid from Florence will ever get into any college again if we continue writing these articles. He called us troublemakers."

"It's all Coleman's fault," someone whined.

"That's right. Kill the messenger!" growled Slick.

"What do you mean?"

"It's an old tradition. Goes way back in history. When a messenger brought bad news to a king, the messenger was killed," Slick explained.

"That's stupid. News is news."

"We can't be blamed for telling the truth."

"Yes, we can. Do you think it's true about getting into a college?"

"Personally, I'm going to save copies of everything we've

printed and include them in my college applications," said Brenda.

"You'll wind up going to school in a foreign country. Besides, you're just a freshman, aren't you. Why should you worry? You have years to erase your record. I'm a junior. My future is closing in on me."

"You know, I forgot that she's just a freshman. I can't believe that I've been following the insane ideas of a stupid freshman. No wonder I'm in trouble. I had myself convinced Brenda was a short upperclassman."

"She's right. It's all Brenda's fault."

"What's her fault?" I asked. "The article was a success."

"You tricked us, Brenda. No real freshman is as bossy as you are."

"And no real senior is as wimpy as you are." I was getting pretty angry. "You know this isn't school, so what does it matter what grade we're in."

"Can you believe this?" shouted Charles. "What's wrong with all of you? A few parents get a little upset and you all start caving in."

"It's more than a few parents," said Lawrence quietly.

"My dad is proud of me," announced Coleman.

"Well, goody for you, peewee."

Before Coleman's protector could do damage to the last speaker, Brenda stood up.

"Since the school year is just about finished, I suggest that we discontinue the *Florence Free Press*—temporarily, of course."

"Of course."

"Sure."

"I'll miss it."

"Me, too."

"Follow me," demanded Brenda. Despite the complaints about her bossiness and age, everyone followed Brenda to the Tuna patio. There we found Mr. and Mrs. Tuna standing near tables that were piled with every kind of picnic treat a kid might like to eat. There wasn't a lump of goat cheese in sight.

"Surprise!" shouted the Tuna family.

"What's this?" asked a sheepish-looking complainer.

"My parents received so many phone calls from your parents last week that I figured the *Free Press* would have to become a thing of the past—temporarily, of course."

"Of course," we all said.

"So I decided to give the old girl a proper farewell—a real good-bye party."

"This is a party?"

"I hate parties."

"I didn't bring a date."

"It isn't that kind of party. It's only noon."

"What does the time have to do with it?"

"I'm not dressed."

"Yes, you are."

"There are freshmen here. If anyone finds out I've been to a party with freshmen, my social life will be ruined."

"What social life?"

As soon as Brenda said party, people started moving apart. The senior girls clustered in one corner with the junior girls near them. The junior and senior boys grouped themselves near the food tables. The sophomore girls inched their way toward the junior and senior boys. The lone sophomore boy stood his ground, looking first at the sophomore girls and then at the freshmen girls. Brenda and I were, of course, the freshmen girls.

"Look what you've done," I said.

"What did I do?"

"You said the word *party* and ruined everything. You overestimated the social development of the staff."

"Ex-staff. I never realized that fourteen kids could form so many groups. It's interesting."

"It's awful," I said.

"It's stupid," said Slick, who with The Boys had formed another group.

"It's a disaster," said Mrs. Tuna, looking sadly at all the beautiful, untouched food.

Brenda jumped onto a chair and whistled. She had everyone's attention. "This is not a party. This is the final meeting of the *Florence Free Press*. Please come to order. Are there any motions?"

Slick raised his hand. "I move we eat."

"I second the motion," I said.

"Any objections?" asked Brenda.

We cleaned off every platter. When everyone else had gone home, Brenda and I sat under a tree and talked.

"I think it was really the horse funeral that did it, Brenda."

"Did what?"

"Finished off the *Free Press*. It was just too strange for most of the parents to take."

"Maybe. It was also the publicity. Florence is a town of appearances. Slick was right. Nobody likes bad news. They killed the messenger."

"Are you sad?" I asked.

"No. Are you?"

"No. I've just been thinking about what we're going to do next year."

"What do you mean by *do*, India?"

"I'm not sure yet. Any ideas, Brenda?"

"Not yet, but I'm sure one will occur to me."

SIXTEEN

THIS was the conversation I had with my family after I was once again invited to travel with the Tuna family for the summer.

"Isn't it great, they're staying in the United States. That means I can go, right?"

"Wrong. Their trip is to Alaska—to camp in the wilderness—among bears and vicious mosquitoes and wolves." My mother was being unreasonable. "It's just not safe. Safe is a nice cabin on Lake George—near a grocery store."

"And a telephone," Rain added.

"I thought you weren't speaking to me ever again," I said to my sister. Rain had made that vow right after the horsemeat story became public. The story had made her sick and had somehow embarrassed her. Rain really believed in blaming the messenger.

"I am speaking *at* her and not *to* her," Rain said to my mother.

"Leave me out of your sibling rivalry and let me finish. . . ."

"What do you mean by vicious mosquitoes, Mom? Do they pick up their victims and carry them away to drink their blood in private?" Smoke was making a horrible face and twisting his fingers in the air.

"Stay out of this, Smoke," I said.

"That's disgusting," said Rain.

"As disgusting as *juicy grilled horsemeat?*" Smoke hunched himself over, rolled his eyes, and came at Rain in a sideways shuffle.

"Keep him away from me!" Rain screamed as she backed away from Smoke.

"ENOUGH!" my mother shouted. "Now, where was I?"

"You were talking about vicious mosquitoes," said Smoke helpfully.

"No, I wasn't."

"You were explaining to India why we will not allow her to go into the Alaskan wilderness with the Tunas." My father was flipping his Sunday morning breakfast specialty—slightly charred pancakes.

"Right. It's too dangerous, India. Besides, a trip with the Tunas would interfere with our surprise plans." My mother winked at my father.

"What surprise plans?" I asked suspiciously.

"How come India is getting a surprise? I want one, too," whined Smoke.

"Maybe you'd better find out what the surprise is before you ask for a piece of it," I warned.

"Breakfast is ready," said my father, placing a large platter of blackened pancakes in the middle of the table.

Rain delicately lifted a single scorched pancake onto her plate. Smoke, who seemed to lack taste buds, stacked his plate with a half dozen. My mother and I, not wanting to hurt my father's feelings, performed our usual Sunday morning act of kindness. We took three pancakes each, drowned them in butter and syrup, and ate them very slowly.

"Oh, yum," I said. "Thank you, Dad."

My father dug into the stack in front of him. "Ahhh," he said, "just the way your grandma used to make them. Takes me back to my childhood—which reminds me of the surprise we have for all of you . . ."

"All of us?" Rain sounded worried.

"Your father and I are going away together for a month." My mother beamed.

"Where are we going?" asked Smoke.

"Not with us," said my father. "Your mother and I haven't spent a vacation alone together since before Rain was born. We need a break."

"You're leaving us home alone? I'll be in charge, naturally. How absolutely great!" Rain was so distracted by the thought of power that she picked a piece of bacon off the serving platter and popped it in her mouth.

"Ohhhh, crispy horse bacon," whispered Smoke. Rain spit the meat into her napkin.

"Alone?" My mother looked amused. "We may be tired. We may need a break from the three of you, but we're not crazy. We are sending you to camp. Isn't that wonderful?"

"I'm too old for camp!" Rain and I shouted.

"Nonsense. Rain is going to be a junior counselor. India is going to be in the senior bunk, and Smoke is going to the brother camp across the lake."

"Counselor? I'll be in charge of people? Brother camp? Are there boy junior counselors?" Rain was interested.

"A lake—that's great. Can I fish? Can I canoe? Can I sleep in a tent?" Smoke was happy.

"I'm too old to go to camp," I insisted.

"You'll all love it so much." My mother wasn't hearing me.

"I'll hate it. You can't just ship me out to camp like a prisoner. I won't go."

"You have no choice." My father had finished his pancakes. He was grinning his deadly grin at me.

"Human beings always have choices, except in situations where oppression is the rule of law," I said.

"The Philosopher's been mucking around with her brain again," said Rain.

"That is my own idea," I lied.

"Then consider yourself oppressed. You are going to camp, not to Alaska. Your mother has a list of what each of you will need to pack. You're leaving on the bus Wednesday."

"My life turns to garbage in three days." I pushed my plate aside and slid low in my seat. All the Teidlebaum kids are great sulkers.

"India, here is a schedule of the things you'll get to do at camp. Look." My mother handed me a camp brochure.

"This is the worst moment of my life." I moaned.

"You're being very ungrateful, India," my mother complained.

"She's turned into a real sour ball," said my father.

"Perhaps you should get her some psychological help," suggested Rain. "Are there socials at this camp? How many? When? Do we see the boys every day?"

"India's bent out of shape because you're taking her away from her other half. India and The Philosopher have been cloned to each other. The two-headed girl has been outsmarted by the mad scientist." Smoke laughed a maniacal laugh as he spoke, spewing milk onto the table.

"The word you were looking for is *grafted*, not *cloned*, pinhead, and you are the most disgusting kid in the world. Excuse me," I said. I grabbed the brochure for Camp Pinewoods and ran all the way to Brenda's house.

"I'm ruined. Camp. Like a baby. They didn't even give me a chance to choose the kind of camp I might like—if I liked camp—which I don't. *You* get to see caribou and wolves and deer and moose and bear, and I get to go to a crummy arts-and-crafts shack twice a week to make lanyards."

"What's a lanyard?" asked Brenda.

"I'll make you one right before I kill myself."

"Now, India, it won't be that bad." Mrs. Tuna placed a big bowl of chocolate chip ice cream in front of me.

"How not?" I asked.

"There'll be so much to do that you won't have a minute to think about how miserable you are." Mrs. Tuna gave me a hug.

"Nice try, Mom," said Brenda. "We'll write to each other, okay?"

"How do I address my letters—Brenda Tuna, Blue Tent Next to the Boulder Near the Iceberg on which the Polar Bear Is Sitting, Alaska?"

"We're going to be stopping at different villages at least once a week. I'm giving you an itinerary. What's your camp address?" We exchanged addresses and spent every possible minute of the next two days together.

On Tuesday night Mrs. Tuna sat down with us. "I've been thinking about your problem, India. Since you must go to camp, why don't you make a meditative experience of it?"

"How?" I asked, not really knowing what she was talking about.

"Well, each week you pick an activity such as archery or swimming or an object in nature, such as a particular tree or kind of plant, and focus your entire attention on it." Mrs. Tuna stopped talking and went over to her loom. I waited for her to continue.

When she didn't, I asked, "And . . . ?"

" . . . and after you learn to focus, your entire sense of the world becomes heightened. Everything around you is clearer. You create Zen camp for yourself. It will make your summer fly by." Mrs. Tuna went back to her weaving. Brenda and I wandered outside.

"Do you know what your mother was talking about?" I asked.

"Sort of. You meditate on something. Concentrate fully on it—with your entire being. Absorb it. Let it become you. You become it."

"I'm not sure I want to become a tree."

"It's probably better than being a camper."

"Probably."

"By the way, India, it just occurred to me—you've finally made it to senior."

"I have?"

"Sure, senior camper, bunk fourteen."

"I hope you have to eat blubber for breakfast every day of the summer, Brenda."

On Wednesday morning, Brenda showed up at the bus depot with her parents.

"This stinks," I complained.

"It's only for a month," my mother reassured me. My parents were looking extremely happy for two people about to send their three beloved children away from home for the first time.

"Aren't you going to miss us?" I asked.

"Of course." They both tried looking sad. It didn't work.

"I'LL MISS YOU!" shouted Brenda as the bus pulled away.

"ME, TOO," I shouted back at her. I kept my face pressed against the window until I could control the tears. I wasn't about to let any of my fellow campers think I was homesick. After all, as Brenda had said, I was finally a senior. I had my dignity to uphold.

Being at Camp Pinewoods was something like being at a strict school—or maybe a military training camp. The days were divided into time periods. Each bunk got a schedule. At the end of each period, your group moved to the next scheduled activity.

There was no choice. If a kid hated softball, tough luck, because at ten-forty-five on Tuesdays and Thursdays you played softball. If a kid loved to read books, tough luck, because there wasn't a single book-reading period in the schedule. Every morning at seven o'clock, a scratchy recording of a bugle playing reveille was blasted over the public-address system. The last official sound at night was the same screaming bugle playing taps.

Every minute of every day was accounted for by some kind of planned activity. The strangest thing was that most of the kids appeared to enjoy being herded mindlessly from one pastime to another.

I mailed my first postcard to Brenda on the second day of camp.

> Dear Brenda,
>   Television has created a generation of zombies and they're all at camp with me. However, I am holding on to my sanity. I have chosen swimming as my first Zen project because we get to swim twice a day every day and I'll have plenty of time to practice. If I become a fish, I will hold your mother responsible.
>   Love,
>   India

By the end of the week, I sent another card to Brenda.

> Tell your mom Zen Swimming is great. I think I will try Zen Pine Trees next because they are everywhere and I can be in sight of one at all times.
>
>   Love,
>   India

At the end of the month, I had mastered Zen Swimming, Zen Pine Trees, and Zen Archery. I failed miserably at Zen Social

Life. I figured three out of four Zen successes were pretty good. I had received a number of postcards from Brenda complaining about the millions of giant mosquitoes and the dangerous thousand-pound bears—both Polar and Kodiak. She wanted to know if her parents were trying to give her a message by always taking her places where she could literally get eaten.

I knew Brenda was just trying to make me feel better about not being with the Tunas. When I arrived home, there was a letter waiting for me. Brenda had written "PRIVATE and PERSONAL" on the envelope.

India—

Write to the Department of the Interior in Washington, D.C., and find out how one goes about adopting a bison from them. It is urgent and important that you do this. It is also *secret*. Do not fail me. I'll explain when I see you. This is the last letter I'll be able to send this summer. Tomorrow we begin a two-week kayak voyage into the wilderness. See you soon, I hope.

Love,
Brenda

Deep down I knew that if I wrote the letter for Brenda, I would be a party to something I might later regret. On the other hand, I was sure that whatever she had in mind would not be boring. So I did it. Two days before Brenda arrived back in Florence, I got my reply. After reading it carefully, I sealed it with tape and hid it in my bottom dresser drawer.

Too bad, I thought to myself. The Tunas just do not have enough space for a bison.

△ △ △

SEVENTEEN

"I'M back!" The screen door slammed behind her as Brenda stormed into our kitchen.

"Oh, goody," said Rain.

"Welcome home, Philosopher," said my father. "Help yourself to some pancakes."

"Is it Sunday already? I sort of lost track of time in the midnight sun. Thanks, Mr. Teidlebaum, those pancakes look delicious, but India and I have our traditional reunion breakfast planned at the diner."

"I didn't expect you for another week," I said, gratefully getting up from the table and heading for my friend. "Glad to see you in one piece."

"What are those red bumps covering your body, Brenda? Have you contracted something contagious?" My mother was holding my arm so I couldn't get to Brenda.

"These bumps are the result of me being bitten by the biggest, meanest, fastest, strongest, most vicious mosquitoes in the world." Brenda winked at me. I began giggling.

"See," said my mother, "I was right."

"Doesn't your family know anything about mosquito repellent?" asked Smoke.

"We lost our supply of repellent when the bear ripped a hole in my father's kayak last week. Let's go, India." Brenda grabbed my hand and pulled me toward the door.

"What bear?" My mother was pale.

"Was your father hurt? Is he all right now?" My father and Mr. Tuna had become pretty good friends.

"He wasn't in the kayak when the bear attacked it. The reason we came home a little earlier than expected is that my father was complaining he couldn't enjoy the scenery from the bottom of my mother's kayak."

"Why was he on the bottom of your mother's kayak?" my mother asked.

"Technically it's *in* the bottom of a kayak, since a kayak is an enclosed boat. It was the only way our kayaks would hold more than one person and they were our only mode of transportation. His choice was to be stuffed into a kayak bottom or be left behind."

"Does anyone here realize that we are pretending to have a rational conversation with the lunatic daughter of lunatics?" said Rain.

"Why are you such an intolerant, narrow-minded, dimwitted, rude, slothlike, pea-brained . . ."

"That's enough, India, I'll handle this," said my mother. "Rain, apologize to The Philosopher immediately."

Rain took a quick look at my mother's face and said, "I'm sorry, Philosopher."

"Apology accepted."

We left the house as quickly as possible. As soon as we were out of earshot, Brenda asked, "Did you get the information for me?"

"Sure I did, but it's not necessarily going to make you happy."

"Why?"

"Because you don't have the minimum amount of land needed to adopt a bison from the government. Their rules are pretty strict. Besides, have you checked this out with your family?"

Brenda started laughing. She giggled, snorted, guffawed, and hooted all the way to the diner. It was embarrassing. I figured that she had had one too many days exposed to the midnight sun. I wondered if there was a medical condition called Arctic sunstroke.

"You should have worn a hat in Alaska. I'm not going in with you until you shut up," I announced.

"You don't have a clue, do you, India?" Brenda gasped between laughs.

"About what?"

"About our plans for this coming year."

"What plans?"

"The ones that include the bison."

"Those must be your plans, since I know nothing about them." I was bugged.

"Don't be silly. All such plans are *our* plans. Aren't we best friends?"

"Maybe you should refresh my memory about *our* plans before I answer that question."

"Let's go inside. The others will be waiting." Brenda ran up the diner steps and headed for a table in the darkest corner. There waiting for us were Slick and The Boys, Charles, and Coleman, who seemed to have grown at least a foot since I last saw him.

"Our carefully chosen inner circle," announced Brenda as she flopped into a chair. "I called them before leaving for your house."

"What's all this about, India?" I didn't recognize Coleman's voice at first. It had dropped about two octaves.

"I have no idea. As far as I knew this was going to be a private reunion breakfast. Ask the certifiable maniac next to me."

Coleman turned to Brenda. "What's this all about?"

"Let's order first," suggested Brenda.

We pooled our money and ordered the Sunday Morning Family Breakfast Feast—more food than an ordinary family of ten can consume but just about enough for seven teenagers. When the pace of eating slowed down a little, conversation resumed.

"You do all realize that we need an interesting project for the year," said Brenda.

"Sounds like the old curse," said Coleman between bites of pancakes.

"What old curse?"

"The one that goes, 'May you live in interesting times.'" Coleman took another piece of toast.

"Why is that a curse?" asked Brenda.

"Naturally *you* wouldn't understand it," he said, "because you thrive on trouble, disaster, excitement, and uncertainty."

"Naturally," she said.

"You might as well just tell us what's on your devious mind, Brenda," said Slick.

Brenda cleared her throat, looked at each one of us, and announced, "We're going to form the Florence High School Booster Club."

She sat back and waited for our reaction. Hands kept moving food from plates to faces, mouths kept chewing, all eyes stared at Brenda.

"Well?" she asked impatiently. "Say something."

"What about the bi—" Brenda kicked me in the shin, hard. "Ouch!" I complained.

"Let's just take it one step at a time, India," she warned.

"Easy for you to say. I might never walk again."

Finally one of the stunned Boys said, "Booster club?"

"A club that exists for one reason only—to support the athletic teams in an institution," Brenda explained.

"I know what a booster club is. I'm just not making the connection," said The Boy.

"Between what?"

"Between you—and us—and it."

"Yeah," said the other Boy. "You hate sports."

"No, I don't, I've just never been very interested in them," said Brenda. "Now I have a reason."

"Ah-ha!" said Slick. "There had to be an ulterior motive."

I began seeing where Brenda was leading her unsuspecting friends. "Oh, no!" I moaned quietly.

"Figured it out, didn't you, India?" she whispered to me. I nodded. She smiled and began speaking.

"This school has cheerleaders, pom-pom girls, drum majors and majorettes, a marching band, twirlers—everything but a booster club and what a booster club can provide for the entire school."

"What's that?" I asked innocently.

"The buffalo," she answered.

"What buffalo?" they all asked.

"The free buffalo the booster club is going to get as a mascot for our school teams, who, as you know, are all called the Florence Buffalos."

"Maybe an Eskimo shaman gave her a powerful potion and she's still hallucinating," suggested Coleman.

"India has already researched the project—it's not just possible, it's a certainty that we can be successful," Brenda lied.

Before I could protest, people began expressing their opinions.

"Nuts."

"Crazy."

"Why?"

"Why not?"

"It's weird."

"Bizarre."

"A buffalo?"

"Like a bison?"

"Just like a bison."

"With horns?"

"With a hump?"

"Camels have humps."

"So do buffalo."

"Bison."

"The hump is their shoulders."

"It looks like a hump to me."

"You're not kidding us, Brenda? A buffalo? Here?"

"Complete with buffalo chips?"

"Are those like potato chips?"

"Or buffalo chicken wings?"

"That's disgusting."

"Will it shuffle off?"

"Do we order it from a catalog?"

"Or a buffalog?"

The smart remarks flew. This did not seem like a serious project. Slick began to chuckle. Charles started to laugh. The Boys joined in with strange donkeyish sounds, and finally Brenda and I couldn't hold out a moment longer. The six of us were out of control. Only Coleman stayed soberly unmoved as he finished the food on our plates.

"I love it." Slick was coughing and laughing.

"Me, too," howled Charles.

"A buffalo," sobbed one of The Boys.

"Where do we get one?" asked the other.

The waitress slapped the check on the table and nervously hurried away. We began to calm down.

"Where do we keep it?" asked Slick.

"You did say it was free. Does someone give it to us or do we kidnap it?" asked one of The Boys.

"Buffalonap it," said the other.

"Maybe it's up for adoption at the SPCA."

"The bison is not exactly free," I said. "There are a few fees we have to pay."

"Fees? You should have said something," said Brenda.

"I am saying something. You should have read the letter before making the announcement."

"This is not a serious project," said Coleman.

"I was thinking the same thing," I said.

"So what?" said Charles.

"So nothing, it was just an observation," I said.

"It is, too, serious, especially now that the booster club is going to have to come up with some money," said Brenda.

"How much money?" asked Charles.

"It hardly matters," I said. "The government hasn't said we could have the bison. They have rules and regulations—strict requirements—which we do not in any way meet."

"What government?"

"The United States government."

"It's the government's bison? Why does the government want to get rid of it?"

"It's surplus."

"Our government has surplus bison? Why?"

"Why does our government have any bison at all?"

"Why don't you know anything about American history?"

We left the diner and walked to my house where I got the

hidden letter from the Department of the Interior. We'd begun to discuss a possible plan of action when we caught Smoke hiding behind a bush listening to us. He didn't respond to threats or bribes so we went to Brenda's house.

"Why didn't you invite the other kids from the *Free Press* to join us?" asked Charles.

"Well, it would be too risky for the seniors—and besides, most of them won't have the time with homework, college applications, college board exams, job hunting. As for the rest of them, they weren't suitably adventuresome or bright," said Brenda.

"Some of them turned you down, didn't they?" I whispered to Brenda. She ignored me.

"I suppose I should feel flattered at being chosen," said Coleman.

"You bet," said Slick.

"Then why do I feel as if I'm standing at the edge of a deep, dark pit?" Coleman asked.

"The feeling goes away after a day or so," I said.

"How do you know?"

"Because I always feel that way when I first get involved in one of Brenda's projects."

"Have you ever fallen into the pit?" he asked.

"There's always a first time," I said. "According to Zen philosophy, even that would be an interesting experience if you were paying attention on the way down."

"Zen?" Coleman asked.

"Maybe one of these days I'll teach you to be a fish," I said.

"You're getting as weird as Brenda, India," Coleman said.

"Probably. How come you're not shy anymore?"

"I grew."

△ △ △

EIGHTEEN

WE had three weeks of summer to complete our preparations. There were two tricky hurdles we had to overcome. The first was getting photographic evidence to show the government that we could provide "an environment suitable for a bison." Brenda wasn't stumped for a minute.

"The football field," she announced.

"What about the white yard lines—they'll know it's a football field and get suspicious," I said.

"You have a whole lot to learn about government bureaucrats," said Charles. "If they're willing to spend seven thousand dollars for a coffee maker, they're not going to pay much attention to some yard lines."

"That was the Department of Defense," I insisted. "We're dealing with entirely different people who probably have their heads screwed on straight."

"Just take the pictures," ordered Brenda.

"Whatever you say, my general." I saluted.

Actually we lucked out. The lines on the football field had been washed away by summer rains. I photographed the grass from all angles. Shooting from the top of the bleachers, I even got what would appear to be an aerial view. Coleman took snapshots of the chain-link fences and of the gates. The whole effort took about two hours.

"Now what?" asked Charles.

"We need some school stationery," said Brenda.

"Terrific," I said. "Project ended."

"Not necessarily. I've made an appointment with Mr.

110

Bingham. We meet him tomorrow at one o'clock. I do the talking," said Brenda.

"I'm getting that feeling again," said Coleman. "I thought you told me it goes away."

"Actually, it comes and goes—but it's not really fatal," I said.

"What feeling?" asked Brenda.

"Never mind. Why are we meeting with Bingham?"

"To discuss the formation of the Florence High School Booster Club."

"Why not wait until school starts?"

"Because all clubs are entitled to supplies, which include a certain amount of special school stationery."

"I forgot that," said Charles. "But what makes you think Bingham will let us be an official club?"

"I'm irresistible."

The next day was the hottest day of the summer. By noon, the temperature had reached 101 degrees. At one o'clock we were standing in front of Mr. Bingham's secretary, Miss Wald.

"You kids picked some day to talk to Mr. Bingham. He hates hot weather and his air conditioner is not working. I'll let him know you're here."

"Enter!" Bingham shouted through his open door.

"Oh, boy," I said. "Let's go swimming and forget this."

Brenda pushed past me. We followed her into Bingham's hot office. He was in his shirt sleeves. A fan was sitting on his desk, blowing into his face.

"What can you delinquents possibly want from me on a day like this?" he groaned.

"We hope you've had a wonderful summer vacation, Mr. Bingham," began Brenda.

"Principals don't get summer vacations, haven't you noticed," he snarled.

"Wonderful start," I whispered. "Real smooth."

Brenda smiled at Bingham and began talking. Maybe, in the end, the heat helped us, because it appeared to me that Brenda simply wore him down. She explained how we were sorry we had caused the school embarrassment with our *Free Press* articles. We had disbanded the newspaper and had decided to reform. We wanted to become part of the official school structure again. Brenda told Bingham we wanted to make it up to the school—get other disaffiliated kids to feel school spirit—promote and organize enthusiasm for school activities—particularly competitive ones. Brenda went on and on. As she spoke, Bingham seemed to wilt. Finally Brenda mentioned the Florence High School Booster Club.

"Booster club, huh?" said Bingham. "What do you want from me at this time?"

"Permission to form the club now so we can order outfits, plan beginning-of-the-term activities, and be ready when the football team plays its first game in September."

"Outfits?" said a surprised Boy. "She never said nothing about outfits."

"Shhhh," I whispered. "It's just part of her spiel, I hope."

"You need a sponsor to be an official club and all the teachers are away," said Bingham as his secretary walked into the office with a glass of ice water for him. "I dehydrate," he explained as he gulped it down.

"I just saw Miss Samansky going to her classroom," said the secretary.

"Why would she be doing that? It's August," said Bingham. "Besides, a booster club needs a different kind of sponsor. Miss Samansky is . . . well . . . not suitable. In addition, she has refused to consider sponsoring any club since the Chamber Music Society fiasco. Give these people an application form to fill out."

To us he said, "Fill out the form and give it to my secretary. When you find a club sponsor, I'll approve the application. Maybe there's some teacher around who'd be willing to take on you problem children. Personally, after last year, I doubt if you'll find anyone willing to put his or her career on the line working with you. Dismissed!" Bingham turned back to his fan. We left the office as quickly as possible.

"Maybe there's some message in this," I suggested.

"What Chamber Music Society fiasco?" said Charles.

"Who's this Samansky?" asked Coleman.

"Didn't you hear him, she's not suitable," I said.

"In Bingham's opinion. Miss Samansky might be the perfect sponsor for us. At any rate, she's our only chance. Where's her classroom?" asked Brenda.

"It's upstairs," said one of The Boys.

"How do you know?" asked Coleman.

"Mrffghe shdnc slerhn wddf her," mumbled The Boy.

"What did you say?"

"He said something!"

"He said he studies jazz trumpet with her."

"You play the trumpet?"

"You know about jazz?"

The Boy nodded.

"You are not what you seem to be," said Brenda.

"Who is?" said Slick.

We had arrived at Miss Samansky's door. Sounds of strange piano music drifted into the hall.

"Her Thelonious Monk tape," said The Boy.

"She teaches religious music?" asked Charles. The Boys grinned and punched each other in the arm.

113

The door swung open. A short, thin, pinch-faced, old woman glared at us. "Who goes there? Or better yet, go away, it's still summer. Or, if you wish, it's summer, so go fly a kite."

"She's nuts." The words popped out of my mouth.

"Hardly, India Ink Teidlebaum. How are you, Howard, have you been practicing? Is that you, Lance, next to David, hiding behind Howard?"

"Who is she talking to?" I asked.

"Slick and The Boys, I think," said Brenda.

"Who's who?" I said.

"Who knows?"

"How does she know who we all are?"

"Beats me."

"I assume you've come here to talk to me. This classroom is as hot as an oven so I was about to leave. If you wish, you may accompany me to my favorite air-conditioned café—providing you have funds to purchase your own food." Miss Samansky locked the classroom door and marched down the hallway. We followed.

"She's strange," I whispered. One of The Boys was violently shaking his head at me and holding his finger over his mouth.

"Don't be stupid, the old lady can't hear her," whispered Coleman. The Boy put his hands to his head as if suffering great pain. Miss Samansky stopped short, whirled around, and glared at Coleman.

"My hearing is in excellent order, Coleman Stern. I advise you to be very careful of what you say around me, especially since I suspect this delegation is about to request a favor."

Not another word was spoken as we followed Miss Samansky to the parking lot. She unlocked a huge, old station wagon, rolled down the windows, and ordered us to get in. We got in.

"Belt up," she snapped, "including the two of you in the rear seats."

We belted. Miss Samansky drove toward the ocean. Twenty minutes later we were seated in a place called Donuts from the Sea. There was sawdust on the floor, the tables were made of wooden hatch covers from ships, the chairs were rickety, and stuffed fish hung on the walls.

"Best air-conditioning on Long Island," said Miss Samansky, studying the menu. "Decide what you want so we can order and get on with our business."

"I'm not really hungry, Miss Samansky," I said.

"Ms. Samansky," she corrected.

"Me, either," said Slick.

"I think I'll try a codfish donut," said Brenda.

"I'll have one shrimp and one clam donut," said Coleman.

"If you order the number five, you get fries and slaw with the clam and shrimp combo," rasped a deep voice.

A huge, bearded, bald-headed man with a multicolored tattoo of a sinking ship on his enormous right forearm had walked across the almost empty restaurant without our noticing. He had an order pad in his ham-sized hands.

"Sounds good to me," said Coleman. "Can I have a cola with that?"

"Why not?" said the man.

"Because if you do, I will be sick. How can you even think of eating a donut made out of fish?" I asked.

"Made with fish, not out of fish, little lady. My fish donuts are crispy dumplings filled with the bounty of the sea. A unique experience in gourmet eating," said the large man. "For the novice consumer of fine food, I suggest you try the daily special, a plate of miniature assorted donuts from the sea—with fries."

"We're novices, all right," I said.

"Then miniature donuts it is—five orders." The man wrote the order in his pad. "And what will you have, Cookie?" he said to Ms. Samansky.

"Cookie?" I whispered to The Boy next to me.

"*Shhh,*" he said.

"I think I'll have a cup of clam chowder, since the air-conditioning is delightfully chilling, as usual."

"What kind of chowder do you serve here?" asked Coleman.

"New England, the only kind worth eating."

"I'll try some."

"Me, too," said Slick.

"What the heck, because you're with Ms. Samansky, complimentary clam chowders all around." The man left for the kitchen.

"You might as well tell me what's on your minds," said Ms. Samansky, who was looking neither old nor pinch-faced as she watched the big man walk away.

Brenda once again acted as spokesperson. She gave a word-for-word rendition of the speech that she had tried out on Bingham. She was confident. She was charming. She was convincing.

"I never heard such bat guano in my life," said Ms. Samansky. "Augie!" she called. "Augie, come hear this, it's a riot."

A tattooed arm swung the kitchen door open and the man returned to our table, carrying a tray of cold drinks. Ms. Samansky introduced us. The man was Augustus Caesarez, her best friend and fiancé.

"Can you spare a few minutes, dear, to listen to something wonderful?" she asked.

"Sure, what's up?"

"Repeat your tale to Augie just as you told it to me, Brenda."

A much less confident Brenda gave her speech to Augie. As Brenda spoke, Augie began to chuckle. When she was through, he turned to Ms. Samansky.

"What . . ." he began.

"Augie," she interrupted, "these are children. Watch your language."

"Some children. Are these some of the ones connected with the *Florence Free Press?*"

"How did you know that?" I asked.

"I didn't. I'm a good guesser."

"The *Free Press* has been disbanded." Brenda was losing control of the situation.

"That explains it," said Augie, pulling up a chair and joining us. "On to a new project, right, guys? What's the scam? Why do you really want to form a booster club? Just how do you want to involve my little Cookie here?" He chucked Ms. Samansky under the chin. She blushed.

"Our only goal is to form a booster club, sir," said Brenda in her most innocent voice. Both Augie and Ms. Samansky started laughing. Brenda looked to us for help.

"Right. We don't know what you're talking about—you think we have—what do you call them?—anterior motives?" said Slick.

"Oh, my"—gasped Ms. Samansky—"a table filled with honor students—half of them playing at being stupid and the rest falsely assuming that we are stupid." She took a sip of iced tea and forced herself to stop laughing.

"What honor students?" asked Charles, knowing full well that he had never received a grade lower than an A-minus in his life.

"Yeah, what honor students?" demanded Slick.

"Don't start with me, young man. If you choose to act the tough buffoon with your friends, that's your business, but I am quite familiar with the school records of the bunch of you. And get that cigar out of your mouth. Smoking is a terrible habit to acquire."

"Why are you familiar with our school records?" I asked.

"I have always been interested in bright, rebellious students. I was one myself. I began following your careers after noting your collective impact on the school via the newspaper early last year."

Brenda squinted at Ms. Samansky, who smiled at her. "Are you going to spill the beans, Brenda?"

Brenda sighed and looked around the table.

"Tell her," said The Boys.

"Might as well," I said, figuring it would end the mad project.

"Okay, talk," said Coleman.

Brenda looked Ms. Samansky right in the eye and said, "I refuse to answer on the grounds it might tend to incriminate me."

"You are not in court, young woman. You are in a restaurant," said Ms. Samansky.

Brenda folded her arms across her chest and stared at Ms. Samansky. Ms. Samansky folded her arms across her chest and stared back. Augie left and returned with our food.

"This is stupid. I'm going to eat," said Coleman, his mouth watering at the sight of the crispy fish donuts on his plate.

"He's right. No need to spoil this delightful snack." Ms. Samansky took a taste of her chowder. We all began eating—except Brenda.

"It won't incriminate you if you eat, Brenda," said Augie, winking at Ms. Samansky.

I could see Brenda's nose twitching. I knew my friend hadn't eaten since breakfast and was starving. She picked up her fork and put a miniature fish donut into her mouth.

"Not bad," she pronounced.

"Ah, my life is complete—'not bad'—the goal of every fine chef in the world—to hear a customer say 'not bad.' It feels as if she actually said—almost good."

"I'm sorry, Mr. Caesarez, the donuts are really pretty terrific," amended Brenda.

"'Pretty terrific'—is that the same as very good?" Augie asked. "And call me Augie—all of you."

"It's the same as great, Augie," said Brenda, starting to relax.

"Ah, my customer says my donuts are great. . . ."

"Enough of this," said Ms. Samansky. "I have made my decision."

"You have?"

"Here comes the end of it," I whispered to Coleman.

"As far as I can tell, you are all about to embark on a scheme that will most probably get you into a great deal of trouble. I could cross-examine you privately and wring the truth from one or more of you, but I choose not to do that. I could refuse to be your club sponsor knowing that, with your reputations for finding trouble, no other teacher would go near you. I choose not to do that, either.

"I am not a fan of sporting events, so for me to be club sponsor to a booster club is a bit absurd—however, I enjoy the absurd. Since I plan for this to be my last year of teaching at Florence High School, I am not much worried about what associating with you will do to my career.

"There are a number of other more personal reasons that influence me to make this decision, but they are none of your business. I shall be your club sponsor. Did you bring the papers for me to sign?"

"I hope you know what you're doing, Cookie," said Augie.

"Not completely—but living life is like playing a jazz set—one feels the inspiration and improvises as one goes along."

"I could get to like you," said Brenda, handing Ms. Samansky the sponsorship papers.

"You wouldn't be the first," said Ms. Samansky.

"By no means," said Augie.

▽ ▽ ▽

NINETEEN

THE next day, after giving our signed sponsor form to Mr. Bingham, we received a Florence High School Official Club Packet. It included the stationery and envelopes we had been waiting for. We were also assigned a school post office box.

"This is all highly suspect," mumbled Mr. Bingham. "I can't imagine why Miss Samansky would want to sponsor a booster club."

"Ms. Samansky," corrected Brenda.

"Whatever," said Mr. Bingham as he wandered back into his office.

"We're finally official," said Brenda.

"Not really," said Coleman. "It says here that we have to submit a club constitution and a list of officers before we plan any club activities."

We went to Brenda's house, where we held the first official meeting of the Florence High School Booster Club. We chose a club name (the Buffalo Boosters), wrote a very brief constitution (three paragraphs), and elected officers (there were just enough positions to go around). This took a half hour.

We then composed a letter to the Department of the Interior, Bureau of Land Management, requesting a bison. Charles, who was the best typist in the group, made the final copy on our letterhead stationery.

"What we have to consider is the possibility that we're perpetrating a fraud," said Coleman.

"Stuff it, Coleman," said a Boy.

"We're going to pay for the beast," said Slick.

"But we're ordering it in the name of the school," said Coleman.

"No, we're not. We're ordering it in the name of the school's official booster club, which is us. Now, where are the photos of the field and fences?" Brenda sealed the photos and letter in their envelope and went to hunt for some stamps.

"They'll never fall for it," I said confidently.

During the next two weeks, we discussed possible booster club projects, but mostly we hung out together. One of us checked our school post office box every day. Three days before the start of school, the letter arrived. I delivered it into Brenda's hands, unopened.

"This is it!" Brenda was practically shaking with happiness as she ripped the envelope. She read the letter to herself and then said, "Uh-oh."

"Snag," I said.

"I told you so," said Coleman.

"No, you didn't. *I* told you so," I said.

"Read us the letter, Brenda," Slick coaxed. Brenda had scrunched herself into a depressed human lump in the corner of our booth at the Chic Chili Pepper.

"I have to think," she mumbled.

"Read it to us and we'll think together," I said, finishing my taco.

"You eating that?" asked Coleman, pointing to Brenda's bowl of chili. She shook her head. Coleman helped himself to Brenda's lunch.

"You're a bottomless pit," I said.

Coleman nodded and kept eating.

Slick had taken the letter from Brenda. "It says that the bison will cost us two hundred dollars . . ." he began.

"I thought the bison was supposed to be free," said Charles.

"It is, technically. That's a processing fee that covers the cost of getting the bison off the range, veterinarian services, paperwork, et cetera," said Slick.

"I thought you told us there would only be a *small* fee, India." Brenda was turning on me.

"I never said *small*. The first letter wasn't specific."

"Then there's transportation," added Slick.

"What transportation?" asked Coleman.

"Did you think they were going to hand the bison our address and tell it to hitchhike here?" I asked.

"Maybe we can send it a bus ticket," said a Boy.

"Or tell it to take a taxi," said the other Boy.

"I hear the train ride cross-country is very nice."

"How about we buy it a bicycle?"

"Or four skateboards."

"It can manage on two."

"Get serious," said Brenda. "We have to hire a trucking firm. There's a list in the letter."

"With what?" I asked. "We pooled our money the other day and all we came up with was twenty-six dollars."

"We're sitting in a restaurant eating. That costs money.

122

We have to begin to make sacrifices." Brenda was getting desperate.

"How far will twenty-six dollars get the buffalo?"

"Maybe as far as Kansas."

"Where is Kansas?"

"Over the Rainbow."

"Wrong, it's over Oklahoma."

"Underneath Nebraska."

"To the right of Colorado."

"It depends on where you're standing."

"STOP!" shouted Brenda. She had unscrunched herself. Her face was bright red. Her fists were clenched. Every head in the restaurant turned to look at us.

"Let's get her out of here," I said. We lifted Brenda out of her seat and dragged her to Slick's car.

"I'm okay now. You can let go of me. I have an idea."

"Do you believe her?" asked Charles.

"About being okay or about the idea?" I asked.

"Let go of me."

"Either. Both. It doesn't matter," said Charles.

Brenda refused to talk about her idea. She made us take her home and then immediately left us in the living room to stew for ten minutes.

"Maybe she's finally snapped."

"Brenda's not the type."

"Sure she is."

"She really wanted that bison."

"She's already got her mind on another project."

"Then where is she?"

"Ta-da!" sang out Brenda. She sauntered into the room, did a couple of turns, and posed, hands on hips, foot on the coffee table. Brenda was in costume.

"What are you wearing, Brenda?" I asked.

"She's a cowboy," said Coleman.

"Cowgirl," corrected a Boy.

"Cowperson," I added.

"I am a member of the Buffalo Boosters. I am wearing the official Buffalo Booster outfit. We are about to embark on a gigantic fund-raising project in order to bring our bison east."

"What official outfit?" asked a nervous Boy.

"The one I mentioned in Bingham's office. Isn't it great?"

"We thought you were kidding," I said.

"I thought you said she had her mind on another project?" said Coleman.

"Sue me. I was wrong," I said.

"No," said the Boys.

"No!" said Slick.

"No, what?" asked Brenda.

"No, we won't wear costumes," said a Boy.

Brenda looked at them and started to laugh. Charles, Coleman, and I, risking our bodily safety, began laughing, too. Slick and The Boys were wearing their usual old jeans, black leather jackets with studded sleeves, spiked belts, and heavy black boots, despite the fact it was summer. Under each open jacket you could see a faded T-shirt with a menacing picture on it. Slick and The Boys looked at each other. The Boys started to smile. Slick took a pipe out of his pocket and shoved it in his mouth.

"Going preppy on us, Slick?" Brenda pointed to the pipe and doubled over with laughter.

"Yeah, I'm getting an alligator tattooed on my chest next week," said Slick, sucking on his unlit pipe. "What we wear are street clothes, not costumes."

"For a member of a motorcycle gang, which you are definitely not," said Brenda.

"Our image will be destroyed," a Boy lamented.

"You can wear a mustache and a wig," I suggested.

"And a false nose."

"And shades."

"No one will recognize you."

While Slick and The Boys sulked, Brenda and Charles dragged several large cartons into the room and opened them. They were filled with western boots in various sizes, suede riding chaps, bright orange neckerchiefs, leather fringed jackets, and large-brimmed, blue-felt cowboy hats with an orange feather stuck in each orange hatband. Coleman, Charles, and I began rummaging to put together outfits in our sizes. Slick and The Boys sat and glared at us.

"I hate orange and blue together," mumbled a Boy.

"They're the school colors."

"I still hate them."

"Spoilsports," said Brenda.

"You're a very pushy broad," said Slick.

"I am *not* a broad."

"*Excuse me.* You're a very pushy person."

"Why don't you listen to my plan?"

"So talk."

Brenda talked and we listened.

"It's not going to work," said Coleman.

"You're getting as negative as India," complained Brenda.

"India is practical, not negative," said Coleman.

"Thank you," I said.

"It will work. Who's with me?" Brenda looked at us anxiously.

I couldn't let down my best friend. I raised my hand.

Coleman was wearing a cowboy hat, chaps, and a fringed jacket. "I kind of like these duds," he twanged.

"Oh, boy." Slick groaned.

"Me, too," said Charles. "I'll do it."

Slick and The Boys were silent.

"We'll do it without you," said Brenda.

"We'll stand by in case you get run out of school," Slick promised.

On the second day of school, having gotten the necessary permission, the Buffalo Boosters set up a booth near the cafeteria. We had used our printing equipment to run off flyers asking the student body to support their teams and participate in the grand event, the big surprise, the Booster Event of Events. We asked each student to contribute generously to the club project as a sign of solidarity. We were confident. We were cheerful. We were Boosters. We were mostly ignored.

That night Mrs. Tuna invited us to dinner.

"At least no one was violent toward us," said Charles.

"May I have some more goat cheese for my salad?" said Coleman. "This is delicious."

"Can't you think of anything except food?" Brenda asked.

"I'm a growing boy," said Coleman.

"If you grow any more you'll be some kind of freak," said Slick, who did not seem to like the attention Mrs. Tuna was giving to the walking appetite.

"How much did you collect?" asked a Boy.

"Eight dollars and sixty-three cents," said Charles.

"Who gave the pennies?"

"Everyone. Ours was not a popular cause."

"Just what is your cause?" asked Mr. Tuna.

"Booster club activities, Dad," said Brenda, not looking him in the eye. "We have to go have a meeting now."

"Our daughter is up to something," said Mrs. Tuna.

"How unusual." Mr. Tuna laughed. "Try not to get yourselves in too much trouble, kids."

We met in the sheep meadow.

"I guess it's over," I said.

"Yeah. We need two hundred dollars for the bison, another several hundred dollars for shipping, money for hay, feed, a bison pen, water bucket . . ." said Charles.

"How do you know all this?" I asked.

"I've been doing research on the care and feeding of an American bison. We need big bucks. Eight dollars will not do it."

"Eight dollars and sixty-three cents."

"Thirty-four dollars and sixty-three cents, if you count what we already had."

"Big deal."

"We need something to get the school behind us," said Brenda.

"I don't feel like being chased out of town," I said.

"Very funny. I could use some support now, India," said Brenda. "When is the first football game?"

"This weekend, on Saturday. Why?"

"Who are we playing?" asked Brenda.

"Great Point High. Why?"

"Perfect," said Brenda.

"I'm getting that feeling again," said Coleman.

"Probably indigestion," I said.

"What's this about, Brenda?" asked Slick.

"The premier appearance of the Buffalo Boosters."

"We've already appeared. Nobody cared."

"This will be our first Booster event—our debut as the heart and soul of Florence High," said Brenda. "After it's over, people will be showering us with money."

"The feeling is getting stronger," said Coleman.

"Try burping," I said.

"Will it be dangerous, Brenda?" I asked.

"Not exactly. Well, possibly. Well, not really dangerous in the usual sense of the word . . ."

"If there's a chance of danger, you'll need us as muscle," said Slick.

"I won't wear chewed leather," said a Boy.

"Chewed leather?"

"That soft stuff the jackets and chaps are made from."

"Doesn't your father have something in his warehouse in basic, motorcycle black?" asked the other Boy.

"Not for cowboys, and we have to be cowboys because of the buffalo," said Brenda.

"Bison. American bison," said Charles.

"As soon as it gets to Florence, it becomes a buffalo," said Brenda, "as in Florence Buffalos."

"Buffalo pull plows and don't have all that fur," said Charles.

"If there really might be trouble, we'll come along," interrupted Slick. "In costume."

The Boys groaned. Brenda took them into the house and gave them their outfits. We spent the rest of the week helping Brenda plan our first booster club event. Friday night we were back at the Chic Chili Pepper.

"We're going to get killed."

"That's better than being ignored."

"Is it?"

"We're going to be heroes."

"Hah!"

"Should we have told Ms. Samansky?"

"She knows something is up," said a Boy. "She told me so."

"How does she know?"

"She says we've been too quiet this week so she's suspicious."

"Do you think we do these weird things because we're nerds looking for attention?" I asked.

"That sounds like something Rain would say," said Brenda.

"It *is* what she said when she saw me at the Boosters' booth on Tuesday."

"Rain's a jerk."

"A twit."

"A pissant."

"A cockroach."

"A bug."

"That's what we've been saying."

"I know."

▽ ▽ ▽

TWENTY

WE met in front of the ticket booth an hour before the game began.

"My boots are too tight," complained a Boy.

"Mine, too," said Slick.

"My dad will bring others home next week," said Brenda.

"You think we're going to do this again? No way," said Slick, fiddling with his neckerchief.

"My toes are losing feeling."

"Don't be such a baby," said Brenda.

The Boy growled at her and stamped his feet. "If I get gangrene, I'm going to sue you."

We walked past the empty ticket booth and headed across the field to the visitors' bleachers. We were carrying two card-board cartons, a rolled-up banner, a bunch of signs, and several Thermos bottles.

"I hope nobody sees us," muttered a Boy.

"Right, nobody will notice seven kids in identical cowboy garb carrying armloads of garbage into enemy territory," I said. "Can't we move faster."

"What for? Hardly anyone is here yet. We're an hour early," said Charles, who was walking with a strange, clownlike, floppy-footed gait.

"Hey, man, are your boots too big for you?" asked a Boy.

"Yes," said Charles.

"Why didn't you say something before this?"

"I wasn't asked."

"Take them off," The Boy ordered.

"Here?" We had reached the edge of the field.

"Now!" ordered The Boy.

"*No!*" commanded Brenda. "Wait until you get to the top."

"Says who?" asked The Boy.

"Says me," said Slick. "It's too dangerous hanging around down here with all this stuff."

We dragged everything to the top row of the bleachers soon to be filled with hostile kids from Great Point High. We took a bright yellow rope from one of the boxes and cordoned off the top three rows of the center aisle—the best seats in our stadium. On it we tied red pieces of cloth and signs saying RESTRICTED AREA—KEEP OUT.

"Kids are starting to arrive. The barbarians are about to overwhelm us," said Coleman.

Angry Great Point fans, having climbed the bleachers to sit in the prime seats, were glaring at us.

"Who made that a restricted area?" demanded one large boy.

"Coach Patrick and Miss Dodd," said Brenda, naming both the head coach and the principal from Great Point. "Foreign dignitaries are coming to see the game. These are their seats. Don't you recognize your school colors—red and yellow?"

"Bull," said the kid as he put one leg over the barrier. "I recognize *your* school colors."

"Hold it!" Slick and The Boys stepped forward. Even in the cowboy outfits, they managed to look tough. Maybe it had something to do with the very real-looking six-guns they had added to their costumes. Slick stood, feet apart, hands just inches from his pistols. The Boys stepped onto a bench and looked down at the kid from Great Point. In a moment both his feet were on his side of the rope.

"It still sounds like bull to me," he said. "Foreign dignitaries . . ." His friends moved toward Slick and The Boys.

"I guess I'll just have to tell you the truth since you're too smart for us," said Brenda, stepping up to the rope. "Come here."

Brenda whispered in the boy's ear. He nodded, smiled at her, and directed his friends to sit where they were.

"What did you tell him?" I whispered to her.

"That some college scouts were coming to see the players on the Great Point team and these were their seats. Much against our will, we have been assigned to reserve the seats for the scouts so they will be able to get the best view of the action on the field."

131

"They believed that?" said an incredulous Coleman.

"Shhh," said Brenda. "Let's get organized."

We sorted out the bags we had packed the night before, got all our equipment in order, and sat down to wait.

"These may be our last few peaceful moments on earth," I said.

"We're going to get killed," said Coleman.

"Maybe, maybe not," said Slick.

"We'll go down fighting," said a Boy.

"Why?" asked Charles. "Maybe we ought to rethink this."

"Too late," said Brenda. "It's the kickoff."

"It's not too late," I insisted.

"Yes, it is," said Brenda. "Now!"

The starting gun went off. The ball flew through the air. It landed in the arms of a Florence High end. The teams began to run. The Boys unrolled the banner we had made and hung it on the tall fence behind us. The play ended, the crowd across the way, our schoolmates, lost their focus of attention and started looking around. Arms began to point toward our bleachers. Kids waved. Others shouted. The cheerleaders saw the banner. They did cartwheels.

There, on top of the Great Point High bleachers, surrounded by the enemy of the day, an enormous sign proclaimed GO, BUFFALOS! WIN, BUFFALOS!

In an attempt to counteract the enthusiasm of the Buffalos fans, the Great Point cheerleaders turned toward the stands to lead a cheer. They noticed our sign. They pointed and shouted at the crowd, but the crowd didn't understand. It was involved with the game. The head cheerleader tried to get the coach's attention, but he was too busy directing his team.

"Our days are numbered," said Coleman.

132

"Our minutes may be numbered," I said, "but it's an awful lot of fun, isn't it?"

"The feeling has gone away," he said.

"It's the adrenaline rushing to your brain. It erases paralyzing fear. Have a bag of confetti." I handed Coleman a bag of orange-and-blue confetti, a whistle, and a noisemaker.

We sat quietly, watching the game. It was going nowhere. By halftime, no one had scored. A number of the Great Point fans had noticed our banner, but by then, the game was so boring, not too many of them cared. We unpacked our snacks and ate watching the Florence High Marching Band, the Florence Twirlers, and the Great Point High Kickers. Nobody on the field seemed to have much spirit.

"It's time to change things," said Brenda, handing us each two tubes.

"What are these, zip guns?" asked a Boy.

"How would you know? They're firecrackers," said Charles.

"Brenda is a pacifist. She doesn't believe in things that explode," I said, examining my two plastic tubes for a trigger mechanism or a fuse.

"Hold one tube in each hand like this. When I give the signal, shake them with a flick of your wrist," Brenda explained.

"But what are they?" asked Slick.

"Magician's equipment."

"If a rabbit jumps out of this thing, I'm going home," said a Boy. "I've been humiliated enough for one day."

"Maybe they'll make us disappear and reappear in a safer place," I said.

"Line up, Boosters. Put the whistles in your mouths."

"Another order from our general."

As the teams ran onto the field, we stood up on the topmost bench—whistles in mouths, plastic tubes at the ready. The cheer-

133

leaders from both sides were knocking themselves out, with little results. A mild "Yay" could be heard over the din of portable radios. When our team was lined up in front of their bench facing us, Brenda said, *"Shake!"*

We blew our whistles as loudly as we could and flicked our wrists. An enormous bouquet of feathers emerged from each tube. We waved the giant orange-and-blue feather clusters high above our heads. The Buffalos saw us. Our schoolmates saw us. The team began clapping each other on the back. The Florence High band struck up the school song. The Great Point band retaliated. Our classmates were going wild. People in the crowd below were not only noticing us, they were giving us nasty, squinty looks and calling us names. The second half had begun.

The Buffalos made a first down. We blew into noisemakers and whistles and waved our feathers. Then a fumble, a recovery, and a Buffalo player outdistanced everyone and scored a touchdown. We had our confetti ready. We threw it in the air and showered the Great Point crowd below us. The kids across the field began laughing and pointing and cheering. The kids below us were about to string us up—old-west style.

"Time to go, Brenda," I warned.

"We have to do the last thing," she said.

"Then let's do it now!" I said.

"She's right," said Slick. "Even we can't hold off three hundred angry football fanatics who are getting uglier by the second."

We unfurled our second banner and held it high above our heads. BUFFALO BOOSTERS. We had identified ourselves. A chant began across the field. It rose in volume until we could hear it clearly, "BOOSTERS. BOOSTERS. BOOSTERS. BOOSTERS." The ball rose into the air. The Buffalos scored another touchdown. The Great Point fans turned on us. We ran for our lives.

As planned, we squeezed under the top row of seats and climbed down the bleacher support structure.

"I can't run in these boots," gasped a Boy.

"Force yourself," said Slick.

"Keep waving the feathers," panted Brenda as we headed toward safe territory. "It's important."

"Eat the feathers," puffed a Boy as he limped past me.

Halfway across the field, just as a gang of strong-looking, furious rich kids from Great Point High were grabbing at the flying fringe of our jackets, we were surrounded by our football team.

"That was fun," said Coleman as a two-hundred-pound player pounded him on the back. "Brenda's like a mad genius."

"Just like," I said.

"You want to go to a movie sometime?" The player who had made the first touchdown was tapping me on the shoulder.

"Who, me?" I asked.

"Yeah," he said.

"Okay."

"See ya," he said, and wandered back to the bench.

All in all, it was a remarkable day. We had survived. Nobody at our school was too mad at us, Florence High won the game, and I had been asked on my first official date—sort of— by a football player.

"So what?" said Brenda.

"So he asked me," I said.

"No, he didn't," said Coleman.

"This is private," I said.

"*This* is how you ask someone for a date. Would you like to go to the movies with me tonight?" said Coleman.

I stared at Coleman. Then I said, "Yes."

"Good, I'll pick you up at seven."

"Fine," I said.

"A perfect match," said Brenda. "The Romance of the Pessimists."

"Eat lint," I said.

"Have fun."

"Thanks."

▽ ▽ ▽

TWENTY-ONE

"MS. SAMANSKY called me this morning," said Brenda.

Brenda had arrived at my house as we were about to sit down to our Sunday pancakes and dragged me into my room.

"What did she want?" I whispered.

"She wanted to know what we were planning. I told her we weren't planning anything—that we had just had a great Booster success at the game. She said 'bat guano' and ordered us to be in her classroom tomorrow after school."

"Maybe we picked the wrong sponsor," I said.

"We picked the only sponsor who was available, didn't we?"

My mother knocked on my door. "What are you two whispering about?"

"We're not whispering," I said.

"Well, it's time to eat. Philosopher, why don't you join us."

Brenda made a face before opening the door. She smiled brightly at my mother. "That would be lovely, Mrs. Teidlebaum."

"No need to lie, dear. You know very well that it's Sunday and we're having pancakes."

"Then I'd be delighted to join you for the company," said Brenda. I gagged.

"India, act your age," said my mother.

"Eat fast," I encouraged Brenda as we entered the kitchen.

"Oh, goody, look who's joining us for breakfast—the Mad Philosopher and her sidekick, the Deranged Cowgirl."

"Rain the Popular. It's such an honor to dine with you," Brenda cooed.

"What is this all about?" asked my father.

"Your daughter and that person embarrassed me twice this week at school. I will *never* be able to face my friends again. *Ever!*"

"What did you do to your sister, India?" My father flipped three pancakes onto a plate and set it in front of Brenda. "For our guest." He beamed.

"Thanks, Mr. T. India didn't do anything to Rain."

"Why don't you let the nerdette defend herself?" complained Rain.

"Don't call your sister names, Rain," said my mother.

I told my family about the public activities of the Buffalo Boosters.

"That's neat," said Smoke. "Can I join?"

"When you're in high school," said Brenda.

"I want to be a Buffalo Booster *now!*" demanded Smoke.

"You can't," I said.

"India had a date with a *boy* last night," Smoke announced loudly.

"She did?" asked Rain. "Who?"

"A date? I thought you were going to the movies with Coleman," said my mother.

"I did."

"Why were you embarrassed by your sister's Booster activities?" asked my father.

"A date? Weren't you in danger yesterday?" said my mother.

"On my *date*?" I asked.

"I think she means at the game," said Brenda, looking amused.

"I want a Booster outfit," yelled Smoke.

"Time to go," I announced. "Thanks for breakfast, Dad, but Brenda and I have Booster business to conduct. We can't hang around." I grabbed Brenda and pulled her out of the room.

"Thanks, India. I don't think I could have handled another mouthful."

"You should have said you had eaten at home."

Nothing much happened that day. We spoke to Slick on the phone. Brenda tried to convince him to join the rest of us in wearing the Booster outfits to school the next day. He said he'd rather be tarred and feathered and run out of town on a rail. He assured us that The Boys felt exactly as he did. In the end, they reached a compromise. Slick promised that he and The Boys would wear the hats.

By second period on Monday, about a hundred kids had congratulated me. I passed Coleman and Charles in the hall but couldn't speak to them. They were surrounded by girls who were fiddling with the fringe on their jackets and grabbing for their cowboy hats.

"Fickle," said Brenda, who had pushed her way through the mob. "Don't forget the meeting this afternoon."

"What meeting?" asked an eavesdropper. "Is it a Buffalo Boosters club meeting? I want to join."

"Me, too," said another kid.

138

"Room three-oh-four. Three o'clock," Brenda shouted. "The first open meeting of the Buffalo Boosters."

"What are you saying, Brenda? Ms. Samansky wanted to talk to us privately, didn't she?"

"You have to learn to grab opportunity when it presents itself." Brenda ducked into her next class.

"Great boots," said a girl. "You Boosters are really hot. Can anyone join?"

"Room three-oh-four. Three o'clock," I found myself saying.

When I arrived at Ms. Samansky's room a few minutes after three, the room was packed with about seventy kids. Brenda was in a corner with Ms. Samansky talking very fast. Ms. Samansky did not look amused. The enthusiastic crowd began stamping their feet and chanting, "BOOSTERS, BOOSTERS." Ms. Samansky made her way through the crush of students, took something from the top drawer of her desk, and climbed onto her desk chair.

"She and Brenda seem cut from the same mold." Coleman had appeared beside me.

"Is that good or bad?" I asked.

An incredibly loud, shrill whistle pierced the air. On the third blast, the room was absolutely quiet.

"That's better," said Ms. Samansky. "I am Ms. Cookie Samansky, the sponsor of the booster club. This is my music room. I trust that you will cause as little damage to it as possible. I understand that this is the first official open meeting of the Buffalo Boosters." Ms. Samansky gave Brenda a dirty look. "The club president, Brenda Tuna, will address you. Madam president . . ." Ms. Samansky stepped off her chair. Brenda took her place.

Brenda began by introducing us, the officers of the club. She deftly handled the problem of names by pointing to The Boys and saying, "Our sergeants at arms, the brave Boys who kept the enemy from overrunning us on Saturday afternoon." The mob yelled its approval.

The next order of business was signing people up.

"This kind of ruins your plans, doesn't it?" I asked.

"This makes everything possible," said Brenda.

"Are you kidding? School rules state that anyone can join any club. We can't say no to a single kid. How do you expect seventy kids to keep a secret?" asked Charles.

"What secret?" asked Brenda.

"The bison, you nit," I said.

"We don't tell them," said Brenda.

"But that's the only reason we started the club," I said.

"We don't tell them that, either. Don't worry about it, I have everything under control." Brenda leaped onto the desk. The new Boosters cheered.

"Fellow Boosters, welcome to the Buffalo Boosters. You are all charter members."

"We want costumes," shouted a kid.

"Yeah. We want costumes just like yours," hollered another.

"Costumes. Costumes. COSTUMES!" The seventy kids yelled in unison.

"Some control," I grumbled to Coleman. "Maybe we had better make our way to the door."

"No way, Miss Teidlebaum." Ms. Samansky grabbed me by the elbow. "You shall stay until the bitter end. There are questions to be answered."

"QUIET!" shouted Brenda. The noise subsided. "These *outfits* are the personal property of the officers of the booster club.

140

There are no club funds to pay for clothing. In fact, there are no club funds at all right now, which is a shame, because we have to find a way to finance club activities including the Big Booster Project."

"We'll pay for our own outfits!"

"Right!"

"Yes!"

"In that case, I will be back in five minutes. India, carry on." Brenda was off the desk and out the door in a flash.

"Carry on?" I asked.

"Go carry on, India. You're the vice president." Coleman was laughing.

I had a shyness relapse. As I faced the roomful of Boosters, my throat closed up. I couldn't say a word. I smiled. They smiled back at me. Finally someone spoke.

"What exactly is the Big Booster Project, India?"

Why me? I thought.

"What a fine question. Do enlighten us, India." Ms. Samansky was smiling at me.

I took a deep breath and began talking. "The Big Booster Project is going to be something that lifts the spirit of the Florence High teams and brings all the students—athletic and nonathletic—together in brotherhood and fun." My voice was shaking. Where was Brenda?

"What does that mean, India?" asked another kid.

"What is the project?"

"Will we all participate?"

"Is it some kind of secret?"

"Tell us."

The crowd was getting unruly. Slick and The Boys had moved next to me. The door flew open, and Brenda was back with us.

"Boosters," she shouted, "arrangements have been made. Tomorrow morning, before school starts, in the main lobby, you will each receive a blue Booster hat with an orange Booster feather in the brim, an orange-and-blue Booster neckerchief, a fringed felt vest, and a collection container. The nominal wholesale cost of the clothing will be twelve dollars per Booster. The containers are complimentary."

The students were on their feet cheering their president. Brenda held her arms in the air. Everyone sat down. "We suggest you make your outfit as authentic as possible by wearing jeans, cowboy boots if you have them, and chaps."

"Where do we get chaps in Florence?" whined some kid.

"We can make them out of felt," suggested another.

"Or not wear them, they're optional," said Slick.

"What are the collection containers for?" someone finally asked.

"To collect money," said Brenda.

"For what?"

"For club activities. We need a treasury, and all Booster activities are for the entire school. The entire school should contribute!" said Brenda.

"That's right!"

"Good idea!"

"What activities?"

"Any activities you decide on—and the First Annual Big Booster Project—to be decided on at a later date."

Committees were formed—a sign committee, a publicity committee, a transportation committee, a supply committee (everyone had liked the confetti and feather wands), a scheduling committee, a communications committee. Each committee elected a chairperson, and the enthusiastic Boosters began planning Booster activities for the weekend football game and mid-week soccer game.

"It's out of our hands now," I said to Brenda as the Boosters swarmed out of the room.

"You have created a monster," said Coleman.

"*We* have created an instant success," said Brenda proudly.

"You've lied to everyone about the Big Booster Project."

"What if they actually collect enough money for the bison?" asked Charles.

"We order it."

"Without telling them?"

"They'll find out soon enough."

"We're going to be sent up the river for embezzlement," said Charles.

"How about for bunko? I think you can get three to five for bunko," added a Boy.

"I like that. Can you see the headlines . . . Buffalo Booster Executive Committee Arrested. Bison Bunko Game Exposed," said the other Boy.

"Don't sweat it. There's always time off for good behavior," said Slick. The males on the Buffalo Booster Executive Committee were laughing and winking and poking each other.

"I give up. Maybe they'll let me share a cell with Brenda."

"Do you really want to?" asked Charles.

"Sure. Who else would I trust to plan a prison break."

Brenda was completely calm. "If you think you're going to get me upset, you're wrong. Everything is working perfectly."

"And just what is everything?" We had forgotten about Ms. Samansky.

"The Booster club, the Booster projects, the outfits—everything," said Brenda.

"And the bison?" asked Ms. Samansky.

"What bison?" Brenda tried looking innocent.

"I have a Spanish quiz tomorrow," said Slick, backing toward the door.

"You do not take Spanish, you take Latin," said Ms. Samansky. "I repeat, and the bison? Exactly what are you up to?"

We were silent.

"A letter came for you today from the Bureau of Land Management. It was addressed to Brenda as president of the booster club. I did not open it; however, I now have a pretty good idea of the trouble you are about to cause." Ms. Samansky did not look angry. In fact, she looked pretty amused as she handed the letter to Brenda.

"You do?" I asked nervously.

"I most certainly do. Perhaps you should have chosen a less astute sponsor." Ms. Samansky was smiling.

"I think we chose the perfect sponsor," said Brenda.

"You're right," said Ms. Samansky. "Contact me when things become impossible. Close the door behind you when you leave." Ms. Samansky left the room singing.

"She knows," I said.

"I told you she was sharp," said a Boy.

"What's in the letter, Brenda?"

"They only have one bison left to ship this season. She's . . ."

"She? We're not getting one of the huge guys?" said a Boy.

"Any bison is big. They want us to telegram them to reserve it if we want it," said Brenda.

"How about payment?"

"The letter says that shipping will probably cost around five hundred dollars—we pay the shipper when the bison arrives.

The government wants its two-hundred-dollar fee up-front. We have to send the money by next Monday." Brenda folded the letter and looked thoughtful.

"That's seven hundred dollars we don't have," said Charles. "But don't worry, I'm sure a public-spirited banker will be happy to give us a bison loan."

"Does anyone have any cash on them? I have to send a telegram," said Brenda.

Nobody moved. "Come on, guys, trust me," pleaded Brenda.

"Why?" I asked.

"Why?" Coleman asked.

"Why?" asked The Boys.

"Why not?" asked Slick.

"My feelings exactly," said Brenda as we emptied our pockets.

▽ ▽ ▽

TWENTY-TWO

I HAD gotten up so early Tuesday morning to help Brenda jam the cartons of Booster outfits into her father's car that my eyes didn't completely open until we got to school. The other Booster officers were waiting for us at the main entrance.

"A big relief," I mumbled to Coleman.

"What is?" he asked.

"You get to carry these in."

Mr. Tuna drove off and I trudged into the lobby. Most of the Boosters were already there waiting impatiently. Every last one of them had on a pair of jeans and a brand-new western-style shirt. There were a number wearing chaps or chaplike imitations made out of felt. Most had on cowboy boots.

"They're here," I said.

"Good observation," said Brenda.

"They're wearing cowboy outfits." I yawned.

"She must be waking up."

"Where did all of you find western-style clothing in Florence?" I asked a nearby Booster.

"We didn't. Last night we went to Dosey Doe Duds in the North Neck Mall and bought out the store," said the girl.

"All of you?"

"Sure."

"That's some dedication—it's thirty miles from here."

"It was nothing for a Booster. Our slogan is No job is too tough for a Booster, no place is too far for a Booster, no goal is too great for a Booster."

"Very catchy," I said. I walked over to Brenda. "They have a slogan," I whispered.

"I heard it. Some want to have it engraved on their belt buckles."

"They'll have to find an engraver who writes in very tiny letters," I said.

We got to work distributing the official Booster paraphernalia. I checked off names; Brenda handed out vests; Coleman, neckerchiefs; Slick fitted hats to heads; Charles collected money; and The Boys made sure each kid left with a collection container. By eight-thirty we were on our way to class.

"That was simple, what's next?" asked a Boy.

"We meet in Samansky's room at three o'clock to count the proceeds," said Brenda confidently.

"What proceeds?" asked Charles, stuffing the money he had

collected into a cloth bag. "This cash belongs to your dad."

"I know that. See you later."

When I arrived at Ms. Samansky's music room just seconds after three, I found Ms. Samansky sitting alone at her desk, facing an empty room.

"What's going on?" I asked her.

"Nothing, obviously. Were you expecting a crowd?" said Ms. Samansky.

"I guess." I was more than a little surprised that no Booster was present. From the moment they had been handed the collection containers, the Boosters had been busy. They were relentless. They would not take no for an answer. I saw them approaching teachers, janitors, visitors to the school, cafeteria personnel, as well as fellow students. If someone said no to a Booster, the Booster would stick to that person, follow him, annoy him, cajole him, bug him until the moment when a defeated hand would reach into a pocket or purse and come up with a donation.

"It's harassment," I said to Brenda during lunch break.

"Isn't it nice that we're not involved," she said.

"Of course we're involved, we're officers of the club. We're responsible. They're worse than cultics at an airport. One of them is going to get punched in the nose."

"Why are you arguing with success?" said Brenda serenely. I gave up.

By three-ten, Coleman, Charles, and The Boys had arrived at Ms. Samansky's room. We sat quietly listening to a Dave Brubeck tape. By three-fifteen, I had chewed the eraser off my pencil.

"I'm going," I announced.

"Maybe they rented a bus with the Booster money and went to Mexico," suggested Charles.

"Maybe they're blowing it on pizza or tacos in town," said a Boy.

Ms. Samansky turned up the volume on her tape recorder and took a pair of drumsticks out of her desk drawer.

"She's good," said Coleman after listening to her execute some very fancy rhythms.

"The best," said a Boy.

"I'm leaving now."

"You said that already, India."

I grabbed my books and began to leave, when I heard shouting in the hallway. Coleman pulled me out of the way just as sixty-five costumed Boosters and Brenda and Slick crowded into the room.

"They were amazing!" shouted Brenda. "They were out at the school buses stirring up the kids and getting them to actually empty their pockets for the Buffalo Boosters."

"These guys are great!" yelled Slick.

"Where is your cool, man," snarled a Boy.

"Yaaay," cheered the Boosters.

The Boosters deposited their day's collection on Ms. Samansky's desk. There was so much money that the kids began to get a little giddy and very silly. The Boys got everyone seated, Coleman and I sorted coins and bills into piles, and Charles counted. By a quarter to four we had our tally.

"Six hundred and sixty-seven dollars." Charles's voice cracked as he made the announcement.

There was a moment of absolute silence while that number sank in, and then the roomful of Boosters went wild. After a few minutes of screaming, jumping up and down, and general celebration, Brenda leaped onto a chair and shouted, "MORE!"

"What is she saying?" I asked Charles.

"She's saying 'more,' " he said.

"I know that. But why is she saying it?"

"You know her better than I."

"MORE! DO IT AGAIN TOMORROW!" shouted Brenda. "Fill up our treasury. DOUBLE IT TOMORROW!"

"More. More. MORE. MORE. Hooray!" The Boosters cheered themselves, took their empty collection containers, and filed out of the room, singing the school fight song.

"You are certifiable," I said to Brenda.

"Why?"

"We have almost enough money to bring the bison here."

"But they don't have enough money for their scheduled Booster projects," said Brenda.

"What scheduled Booster projects?"

"It's interesting how the club seems to have taken on a life of its own," said Brenda. "They've planned Booster events for all major games and are now working on support activities for all Florence High School teams—including the nonathletic ones such as the chess club and the debating team."

"When did they do all of this?" I asked. "They only joined the club yesterday."

"Late last night. They met in the homes of committee chairpeople. They used telephones. They . . ."

"It's a real booster club." Charles sounded surprised.

"It certainly is," said Ms. Samansky. We had once again forgotten she was there.

"Isn't it interesting how the best-laid plans of mice and men often go awry." Ms. Samansky winked at us. "This money should go into a bank today."

"I'm an officer of a real booster club," said Slick. "Brenda, you've ruined my life."

"A few minutes ago you were shouting about how great the Boosters were," I said.

"I didn't fully realize the implications."

"I kind of like it. It's perverse," said a Boy.

"The bank," said Ms. Samansky. "I'm sure you'll also want to get to the post office before five, won't you, Miss Tuna?"

"Why on earth would I want to do that?" asked Brenda as Ms. Samansky left. Then she turned to us and said, "Let's move it."

We opened a Buffalo Boosters account at a local bank by depositing four hundred and fifty dollars. We also bought a bank check in the amount of two hundred dollars and made it out to the Department of the Interior—Bison Project. At the post office Brenda folded the check into a typed letter and carefully placed both into an express mail envelope.

"How come you had the letter written?" asked Coleman.

"I knew everything would work out and that we'd have to move quickly," said Brenda.

"I wonder when our bison will get here," I said.

"I wonder what we'll do with her," said Coleman.

"Bison are not exactly house pets," said Charles.

"There's a whole lot of care she's going to need," said a Boy.

"The only pet I've ever had was a canary."

"I rode a horse once."

"We'll work everything out," insisted Brenda, but for the first time in days, she looked a little nervous.

On Wednesday, the Boosters turned in seven hundred and one dollars. On Thursday they collected five hundred and thirty-six dollars and apologized to each other for having a slow day. On Friday, with the enthusiasm for Saturday's big game at a peak, the Boosters managed to cadge eight hundred and sixteen dollars from their fellow students. They reported that there were kids who had contributed three and four times.

On Friday, after counting the money twice and adding together the daily figures, Charles was too nervous to speak. He wrote the amount on the chalk board: $2,720.42.

Everyone was impressed. The Boosters were congratulating themselves when a Booster shouted.

"How about the Big Booster Project? Do we have enough for it?"

"Absolutely," said Brenda.

"What exactly is the Big Booster Project?"

"Right. When can we get started on it?"

"Let's begin with smaller events and build up to it," said Brenda. "When the time comes that we're ready as a club, we'll execute the project together. Trust me."

"We trust you!" shouted the Boosters.

"I declare the fund-raising ended and the age of Boosterism begun! Long live the Buffalo Boosters!" Brenda tossed her hat in the air. Sixty-five other hats followed. The Boosters left the room in their usual enthusiastic manner.

"That was disgusting," I said.

"What was?" asked Brenda.

"Long live Boosterism. Telling them to trust you. Lying to them about how they would help choose the Big Booster Project."

"I never said that. I told them they would participate and they will. I don't lie, you know that. Now let's get to the bank." Brenda was indignant.

"Before this farce goes any further, I think you and I had better have a talk," said Ms. Samansky.

"We keep forgetting you're around," I said apologetically.

"That's not very flattering, India."

"I didn't mean . . ."

I was interrupted by Miss Wald, Mr. Bingham's secretary, who came rushing into the room, looking harried and bugged. "Miss Tuna, Miss Tuna."

"I'm Brenda Tuna," said Brenda.

"Of the booster club?"

"Of anyplace."

"Then the phone call is for you—from the *government*. The man on the line said it was *very* important—official business, he said. Oh, my, I'm glad I caught you. He wouldn't talk to anyone else—not even to Mr. Bingham."

"Mr. Bingham tried to talk to him?" Brenda asked warily.

"No, no. Mr. Bingham isn't here. But the government man said he had business to conduct with you and the booster club and nobody else. Are you in some sort of trouble?"

"Of course not. I'll take the call. I've been expecting it," fibbed Brenda as she headed for the main office. We all followed at a fast clip.

"Isn't it nice that she never lies," whispered Coleman.

"A paragon of honesty," I said.

Brenda picked up the office phone.

"Yes, sir. No, sir. I'm glad you got our express mail package. Certainly I'm a kid. I'm also president of the Florence High School Booster Club. Of course we have an adult sponsor." From Brenda's end, the conversation did not seem to be going well.

"Well, if you insist, I'll see if I can locate her." Brenda put her hand over the mouthpiece. "He wants to speak to Ms. Samansky," she whispered.

"Give me the phone," ordered Ms. Samansky.

"Samansky here. Now, just what is the problem, Mr. . . . Mr. Thomas. Nice to make your acquaintance. About the problem? . . . Ah, I see. Of course. Naturally. I sympathize. We shall trust your judgment. The shipping address? One-sev-

152

enty-seven Chestnut Drive, Florence. Five-five-five, six-six-one-six. If there is no answer at that number, the truck driver will be able to reach me or a club officer at the school. When might we expect shipment? That soon? Yes, I understand your need for haste. Now, what is the name of the shipper you are using? Thank you. Good-bye." Ms. Samansky hung up the phone and grinned at us. Then she began laughing.

"What's so funny?" I asked.

"I think this is about to become my most exciting year as a teacher."

"What's happening, Ms. Samansky?" prodded Brenda.

"Much. Let's get the money to the bank. After we have done that, you will contact your parents and ask them if they will give permission for you to be my guests for dinner. After dinner, we will discuss this entire matter."

We had finished with the bank and were climbing into Ms. Samansky's car.

"Are we going to your house to eat?" asked Coleman.

"No, Augustus is preparing a meal for us at Donuts from the Sea."

"Does he know about the phone call from the government?" I asked.

"Augustus knows everything."

"I wish I did," complained Brenda.

▽ ▽ ▽

TWENTY-THREE

AUGIE served up a huge platter of fish donuts and fries. While we were stuffing our faces, he and Ms. Samansky sat next to each other, whispering.

"Now will you tell us what the government man said?" Brenda was almost whining.

"You're almost whining, Brenda," said Ms. Samansky.

"I don't whine."

"Mr. Thomas told me that it was necessary to ship the bison immediately since she is the last of the present lot."

"You mean this week?" I asked.

"I mean today."

"I don't think we're ready for this," I said.

"Yes, we are." Brenda had cheered up considerably.

"No, you aren't," said Augie. "Where are you going to keep it? You can't just let it loose on the football field."

"How do you know what we planned?" asked Slick.

"Augustus knows everything," said Ms. Samansky.

"I give up," I said. "Why are you helping us? They're going to fire you. Your reputation will be ruined. You're an adult. This is a stupid kid prank. . . ."

"It is *not* a prank," said Brenda.

"It is not a *stupid* prank," said Ms. Samansky. "In a bizarre way, it's brilliant. As for why we are helping you . . . let's just say we have our personal reasons."

"You're a spy for the administration," said Coleman.

"If that were the case, I would not have provided Mr. Thomas with my address."

"What does your address have to do with anything?"

"The bison will be arriving at my house in about four days. I felt it was unwise to have it unloaded at the school."

"Four days?"

"What will we feed her?"

"Hay."

"Hey, what?"

"Don't be thick, H-A-Y. Hay."

"Where will we get hay?"

"How do we keep the bison from running away? It's not exactly a dog on a leash, it's a wild animal. A big one."

"Now you kids are beginning to think ahead," said Augie. "Let's make plans."

We met at Ms. Samansky's house at eight the following morning. We had decided to convert her garage into a bison stall. While we cleaned out twenty years of accumulated junk, Augie made a couple of trips to a feed store and a lumberyard. Coleman and I manned an impromptu garage sale at the edge of Ms. Samansky's driveway while Augie directed the others in the construction of a heavy-duty fence with a gate. They installed it across the front of the garage, using monster nails to anchor it into the concrete floor.

"That just might hold a bison," Augie said.

"Just might?" asked Slick.

"Probably will," said Augie.

"Probably?" asked The Boys.

"Most likely. Bison are strong. Fortunately, this one is a female—much lighter than a male. When she butts the wall, it will probably hold. Lucky this is a brick garage. An angry bison could ram its way right out of an ordinary wooden garage."

"Butts?"

"Ram!"

"Bison use their huge heads to defend themselves. They lower them, paw the ground, and then charge when they feel threatened," Augie explained.

"It's a good thing we don't want to threaten it," I said. "We want to take care of it."

"I hope the bison understands that," said Augie. "Put a couple of bales of those wood shavings into the stall and stack the hay so it won't get wet if it rains."

When we were through, we closed the garage doors and the bison stall was once again an ordinary brick building on an ordinary street. Nothing happened on Sunday. It was so peaceful that I almost forgot I was the vice president of the richest club in the history of Florence High and a coconspirator in a plot that was going to get me expelled.

On Monday, the entire school was talking about the Buffalo Boosters. While their executive committee had been toiling to make a home for our secret bison, the real Boosters had planned and carried out a spectacular event during the Saturday football game at Rockville Cove. It involved a rather large contingent of Boosters sneaking into the Rockville Cove bleachers disguised as Rockville Cove students. It also involved kettledrums, bass drums, two tubas, and the cooperation of a great many non-Boosters. It was a miracle that nobody got hurt in the mad dash the imposters had to make to their rightful side of the field.

"Running for one's life is becoming a Booster tradition," I said.

"We have created a fabulous organization," mused Brenda.

"It's a *real* booster club," said Slick. "I can't stand it."

"What do you have against school spirit?" asked Charles.

"And success?" asked Brenda.

"And popularity," I said. "Everyone in the school likes and admires us—except Rain, of course. And I'm sure she'd become a Booster if Brenda and I managed to disappear."

"Rebels don't care about simplistic, superficial emotions and activities. Rebels cannot be joiners." Slick stuck a cigar in his mouth.

"You are going to rebel yourself into an early grave," I said. "You smoke too much."

"Smoking will stunt your growth," said Coleman.

156

"Pollute the air around you."

"Pollute the air in you."

"Get you sent home for the day. We're still at school."

"I don't smoke," said Slick.

"Is that an illusion?" I said, pointing to his cigar. "And how about your pipes and fancy black-and-gold foreign cigarettes?"

"Have you ever seen me light up?" asked Slick. "So the answer to your question, India, is yes, it is all an illusion. I do not smoke." Slick looked smug. "A rebel does unexpected things. He makes statements with his dress and actions and manner. There is no reason for a rebel to destroy his life and health in the process. Get it, chickie?"

"Don't call me chickie," I said.

"Rebels don't run booster clubs . . ." said Slick.

"So quit," I interrupted. Brenda hit me in the arm and glowered at me.

". . . but they do order bison from the Department of the Interior and hang out with impossible, irritable, bossy chicks . . ." Brenda hit Slick in the arm.

". . . women." Slick winked at Brenda.

All in all, it was a quiet week at school. By Wednesday, having received no word of our bison in transit, we began getting very nervous. Brenda tried telephoning Mr. Thomas, but he was off on vacation. She called the shipper, who told her that the truck was overdue. As far as the company knew, our bison was on the road somewhere between Montana and New York.

On Friday, Brenda was pulled out of math class by Miss Wald for another urgent telephone call. Brenda insisted that I be taken out of my Spanish class to accompany her, just in case the phone call contained some shocking news.

The call was brief. Brenda said yes a number of times and then gave the person on the other end directions from the Long Island Expressway to Florence to Ms. Samansky's house.

"It was the driver, wasn't it?" I said.

Brenda pulled me into the hallway. "A nasty and obnoxious person. He'll be in Florence between three and five, depending on traffic. He said that if nobody is there to receive the shipment, he's going to dump it on the driveway and leave."

"He's bluffing. We have his money. He's not going to leave without it." I sounded more confident than I felt.

We stopped by Ms. Samansky's class to tell her the news. She said she'd call Augie and he'd get to her house early and wait for the truck. After school we began our bison watch. By four we were getting jumpy. By five we all called our parents and said we were at Ms. Samansky's house for a long meeting. By six we were sure our bison was squashed somewhere on the Long Island Expressway. At six-fifteen, a large truck turned into the street. It pulled up in front of the house. A cursing, sweating truck driver jumped down from the cab with a clipboard in his hand.

"Who's B. Tuna?" he shouted.

"Me," said Brenda.

"You're a kid. Who's going to sign for this cow?"

"It's a bison," corrected Charles.

"Who asked you?" growled the driver.

"Give me the paper and I'll sign it," said Brenda, beginning to lose her temper. "I'm the one you talked to on the phone."

"Where's the Samansky broad I was supposed to talk to?"

Augie stepped forward. He did not look friendly.

"There is no 'Samansky broad' here, buddy. Just give the kid the clipboard and let her sign for the shipment. She's holding your check."

The driver handed the clipboard to Brenda. She began signing the receipt, but Augie stopped her.

"We want to see the shipment first," he said.

"Are you kidding? That thing in there is wild. It's been trying to destroy the inside of my truck since the beginning of the trip. Had a breakdown in Ohio and let the cow into a farmer's field while the truck was in the shop. Took us a whole day to round it up. I don't open that door for no one until I get paid. If it escapes, it's on your head."

"Let's just get her out of there, Augie," Brenda begged. Augie nodded. As Brenda signed four copies of the invoice, the bison began crashing against the walls of the truck.

"Get that meat on the hoof out of there before I have no truck left," shouted the driver.

"Back it into the driveway, right up to the garage," ordered Augie. The driver cursed but complied.

"You have a ramp?" asked Augie.

The driver set up the ramp. "Open the doors," ordered Augie.

The driver opened the doors and leaped back. Nothing happened. We peered into the truck. The water tub had spilled and the entire floor of the truck was covered with soggy hay and manure. The bison was backed into a corner away from the open rear doors. Her head was down and she was staring at us. Suddenly she opened her mouth and bellowed. It was an unearthly sound. We all jumped back.

"She's agitated," said Coleman. "The sounds bison make depend upon their emotional state."

"How do you know?" asked a Boy.

"I've been doing research."

"So how do we get her out of there?"

"Beats me. The largest pet I ever owned was a goldfish."

159

"Big help you are."

In the end we all stepped out of sight and were absolutely quiet as the frightened bison made her way to the rear of the truck, down the ramp, and into the clean stall to the pile of fresh hay. As the ramp was lifted, we closed the stall gate. The bison backed into a corner and stared at us.

"Why doesn't she turn her back to us and try to hide if she's so afraid?" I asked.

"Because she is protecting herself. She is ready to charge us, her enemies, and butt us with her head," said Coleman, our new bison expert. "An angry or defensive bison is extremely dangerous to people on foot or on horseback—if it decides to charge, it can flatten a person. Then it will use its head and horns to maul the victim." Coleman sounded a little bit like Smoke telling a nauseating story.

"Maybe we should have done research sooner," I said.

"Children, our bison needs some peace and quiet. We shall go inside, have some food, and plan our next step carefully." Ms. Samansky was looking at the bison as if it were a tiny, frightened kitten.

We tiptoed away from the nervous beast and went into the safety of the house.

▽ ▽ ▽

TWENTY-FOUR

"I AM originally from the southwest—Arizona," said Ms. Samansky, explaining the heat of the chili she had just served us. We were frantically gulping down tall glasses of ice water.

"The pain goes away after a while," said Augie, who was calmly spooning chili into his mouth. "Cookie, this is delicious."

"Are you also from the southwest?" gasped Coleman, who had attacked the chili with his usual enthusiasm.

"No, from New England. Eating chili is like riding a bicycle. In the beginning you have to learn to balance and pedal and brake and steer—and you always fall off a few times. But once you learn to ride, you never forget. The skill is with you forever."

"Does that mean I'll get used to this stuff?" asked a Boy.

"Probably, if you eat enough of it . . . in time," said Augie.

"How about naming her," said Brenda.

"Naming who?"

"The bison."

"Killer," suggested a Boy.

"Inappropriate," said Brenda.

"Who made you queen?"

"Fang," said the other Boy. Brenda's eyes began to narrow in anger.

"Get serious," she demanded.

"We are serious. Mascot."

"Too simpleminded."

"Thanks."

"Don't mention it."

"Florpgphh," said Brenda. She had finished her painful dinner and had stuffed two ice cubes into her mouth.

"Very musical," I said, "and easy to remember—Florpgphh."

Brenda took the ice cubes out of her mouth. "I said Florence."

"Florence? As in FEH? You want to name that innocent animal after a woman who would happily turn her into buffalo-hide car seat-covers? You astonish me."

Brenda smiled at me. "It's not going to work, India," she said.

"What isn't?"

"Getting me to lose my temper. You know exactly what I meant. Florence Buffalo—as in Florence Senior High School."

"Catchy."

"Original."

"Unique."

"Okay, so it isn't the most fantastic name in the world, but it's good public relations."

"We're sure going to need those."

"We can call her Flo."

We decided to let Flo recover from her terrible trip East by having her live at Ms. Samansky's for a week. By Tuesday afternoon we had made absolutely no progress with the frightened bison. When left alone, she ate her hay, drank water, and slept a whole lot, but whenever a human came anywhere near the stall, she backed into a corner and lowered her head. We were able to open the stall door and clean the part of the stall we could reach with a manure fork, but no one was brave enough to go in with Flo. Even Coleman, who had read every single word in the public library written about bison, was of no help at all.

"This isn't working," I said. "We can't take her to school if she's totally wild—and we can't keep her in a garage for her whole life—she needs running room. Maybe we've made an awful mistake."

"Help is on the way," announced Brenda.

"She's called the cavalry."

"The Royal Canadian Mounted Police."

"The Bronx Zoo."

"The ghost of Buffalo Bill."

"Better than any of those," said Brenda. "I called an expert, and here he is."

162

A silver-haired old man in an expensive-looking suit, carrying a tubular cloth suitcase, was walking briskly up the driveway. His eyes were fixed on Flo.

"You called your grandfather, George Washington Tuna, King of the Weird, to solve this problem?" I whispered to Brenda. Out loud I said, "Hi, Mr. Tuna."

"Hello, Indala darlink. How's by you?" He pinched my cheek and walked over to Flo.

"No disrespect intended, but what does your grandfather know about bison? There are no bison in Rumania, and you've told me that since coming to America he has not been west of the Hudson River." I was watching Mr. Tuna watch the bison. He was really concentrating.

"Ha, Indala," he said without breaking his eye contact with Flo, "you heves got thet absolutnilly rung. Three times I heve beens to News Joisney. Etlentic City, no less. Da solution to your problem is in mine setchel. Takes mine vord. Now I tinks for a moment."

"How do you know about bison, Mr. Tuna?" asked Coleman.

"You're being rude, Coleman," said Ms. Samansky.

"How do yous do, nice lady. I am George Vashington Tuna, grendfather to thet pretty child." Mr. Tuna took Ms. Samansky's extended hand.

"I'm Cookie Samansky, the sponsor of the booster club. This is my fiancé, Augustus Caesarez. Delighted to meet you, Mr. Tuna."

"Likevise, pretty lady." Mr. Tuna raised Ms. Samansky's hand to his lips.

Ms. Samansky blushed. "Very continental," she whispered.

"Thet's me," said Mr. Tuna. "Now lets the childrens asks qvestions."

"Where did you learn about bison, Mr. Tuna?" I asked.

"Yous is a good goirl, Indala, wit a good skepnical mind."

"Skepnical?" I whispered to Brenda.

"Just let him answer your question," Brenda hissed in my ear.

"Bronx Zoo, Indala. Bronx Zoo." George Washington Tuna smiled at me.

"You learned about bison at the Bronx Zoo?"

"Sure, vhys not? Bison, cows, volves, camyels, pachnee-doirms, lions—aneemals vit four feets is aneemals thet sticks together. Just like boirds. Gets it?"

"No," I said.

"Ah," he said. "Maybe yous is just being a true skeptnic."

"Skeptic, Grandpa," Brenda whispered.

"Skeptic, skeptnic, vhatsever. Lets me tink. I heves other adwice to give out today. This place is as noisy as Grend Central Station."

Mr. Tuna went back to staring at Flo. "AH-HA!" he finally shouted. He bent over, rummaged in the large, embroidered cloth bag he called his setchel, and pulled out a white paper sack, which he handed to Brenda. He patted Brenda on the head, lifted his carrier by its wooden handles, kissed Ms. Samansky's hand once again, and said, "No charge for givings adwice to felnow patriotic Americans. Heves a good day." He began walking down the driveway.

Brenda looked inside the paper bag and called after her grandfather, "Wait, Grandpa! What do I do with these? What's your advice?"

"Use your head, Brendala, likes in our old country. Figures it out, Grendchild."

"I was never in the old country, Grandpa," she shouted.

164

"Of course you veren't. So vat else is new? Good lucks, childrens and nice grown-up peoples." Mr. Tuna was out of sight in seconds.

"Expert." I snorted.

"He sure moves fast for an old guy," said Slick.

"Don't make fun of my grandfather. He's always right—at least he has been up until now. His advice is highly sought after." Brenda was angry at me.

"I'm sorry, Brenda. I really like your grandfather but . . ."

"He is likable," said Ms. Samansky before I could put my foot in my mouth again. "What did he give you?"

"Cookies. My mom's oatmeal-raisin cookies—about two dozen of them," said Brenda.

"Maybe he handed you the wrong package," I suggested.

"My grandfather does not make simpleminded mistakes at critical moments. Let me think."

"That's what he said just before he handed you the cookies," said Coleman.

Brenda said something like "haruumph" and went over to Flo's stall. She absentmindedly reached into the paper sack and took out a cookie, which she began to eat. Flo lowered her head and backed into her favorite corner.

After a few minutes, Flo raised her head and sniffed the air. Brenda finished the cookie and began on a second. Flo took a step forward.

"Psst, Brenda, look!" I whispered.

"I see, India." Brenda stuffed the rest of the cookie into her mouth. Flo sniffed the air again and lowered her head.

"*That's* what Grandpa meant!" Brenda said, waving the bag of cookies in the air. "He's a genius. I knew it."

"What?" asked Ms. Samansky.

"The cookies," said Augie.

165

"I'm confused," I said.

"I'll explain," said Brenda. "In the old country, in the olden days, each family had at least one huge, vicious dog guarding its little farm. This was before there were big roads and automobiles and buses. A person walked almost everywhere—unless he or she was lucky enough to own a horse.

"A person going into town—or from his farm to a relative's farm—would naturally have to pass by all those other farms with the vicious dogs." Brenda smiled. She took another cookie out of the bag. Flo looked at her suspiciously. Brenda took a bite. Flo watched her chew.

"Is this going to be some kind of old-country shaggy-dog joke?" asked a Boy.

"Shhhh," I said. "I think maybe she's headed someplace with this."

"Yeah, outer space."

"As you passed each farm with the killer dog guarding the house, the fields, the road, and the surrounding countryside," continued Brenda, "you had several choices. If you were very fast, you could try to outrun the dog. If you were very strong and foolish, you could stand and fight it. If you were desperate, slow, and weak, you could remove all your clothing . . ."

"The old Ukrainian trick!" shouted Augie.

"Grandpa is from Rumania," said Brenda.

"But the trick originated in the Ukraine, or so I've been told," said Augie.

"What trick?" I hollered. "What has all this got to do with Flo?"

"It is said that the sight of a naked human wandering in the countryside so surprises and confuses a dog that by the time the animal recovers, the human is long gone. Not a trick to rely on in winter, however," said Augie.

166

"Not a trick to rely on at all," said Ms. Samansky. "Sounds like a lot of horse manure to me."

"WHAT DOES ANY OF THIS HAVE TO DO WITH FLO?" I screamed at the top of my lungs. Flo put her head in the air and bellowed.

"Sorry, Flo," I said.

Brenda went on as if there had been no interruptions. "The best way for a human to pass unharmed through the hostile territories on foot was to carry a burlap sack of oatmeal-raisin cookies—whole wheat, of course."

"Of course," said Coleman, trying to keep a straight face.

"The dogs could not resist the cookies. The cookies diverted their attention, filled their empty bellies, and tamed them."

"Tamed them? Vicious guard dogs trained to rip apart all intruders? I guess I'm just a skeptnic, Brendala. It all sounds like horse manure to me, too," I said.

"Who said anything about training? These were naturally nasty dogs. The cookies were foolproof. Irresistible. A traveler's only worry was running out of cookies before his destination was reached. Nobody much liked using the other methods of dog avoidance. Now watch."

Brenda took a cookie out of the sack. Flo raised her head. Brenda broke off a piece of cookie and tossed it into the stall right in front of Flo. Flo sniffed it, touched it with her lips, and then sort of sucked it into her mouth. When she had chewed and swallowed the bit of cookie, she licked her lips and stared at the bag in Brenda's hand. Brenda threw her another nibble.

At the end of a half hour, Flo was eating oatmeal-raisin cookies from Brenda's hand. Brenda was stroking Flo on the nose. Brenda sent Slick to her house for more cookies, insisting it was the secret family recipe that did the job.

"The instructions that came with her said we should stick

strictly to simple food like hay, water, grass, and maybe some grain in winter. These cookies might make her sick," said Coleman.

"Impossible. These *are* simple food—completely organic, totally healthful. Here, you feed her one."

That was Tuesday. By Saturday, Florence Buffalo was a contented, semitame bison. She would take cookies from any of us. She no longer challenged us when we went near her stall, and Brenda could actually lean on Flo and scratch her enormous head. All of us except Brenda were a little dazed over our success.

We were giving Flo her evening hay and water and discussing how to move her to the school. We had prefabricated a bison pen, had bought more hay, and had targeted Sunday as bison day.

"Boy, is she fat," said Slick as Flo licked cookie crumbs from his fingers.

"Too many cookies and no exercise," said Coleman. "We're not moving her a moment too soon."

"I wonder," said Ms. Samansky.

"What?" I asked.

"Just a silly thought. Never mind. See you young people tomorrow morning."

"Your grandfather is a smart man, Brenda," said Slick as we walked home.

"Naturally."

"Do those cookies work on all animals?" I asked.

"Four-legged ones and birds. Also many sea mammals."

"What's left?" asked Slick.

"Snakes and fish," said Brenda.

"What does your grandfather say about snakes and fish?" I asked.

"Eat them before they eat you."

"Oh." I walked home munching on an oatmeal-raisin cookie. It was soothing.

▽ ▽ ▽

TWENTY-FIVE

ON Sunday morning, Brenda and I arrived at the Florence High School football field at six-thirty.

"The joggers aren't even up yet." I moaned.

"That's the point. No one will see us."

"Where's the sun?" asked Slick, getting out of his car and yawning loudly.

"At home asleep," I said.

"Here comes Augie's truck," said Brenda. "Help me with the gates."

The rest of the Booster Executives arrived in time to unload the prefabricated bison pen, the water tub, six bales of hay, four bales of shavings, a large toolbox, bags of quick-mix cement, a wheelbarrow, containers of water, and some shovels onto the grass near the field house. We got right to work. We assembled the pen, using the field house as a sheltering wall.

"It will provide shade in hot weather and a wind barrier in the winter," said Augie.

"An optimist," said Ms. Samansky.

"How so?" asked Augie.

"You mentioned winter, Augustus. It is unlikely that the school authorities will allow Flo—or me, for that matter—to continue at this school more than a week or two after this misadventure becomes public," said Ms. Samansky.

"They wouldn't dare fire you," said a Boy.

"Certainly they would. It is a matter of no consequence."

"How can you say that?" said the other Boy.

"Easily. We'll discuss this at a later time. Keep working. We're on a schedule."

We dug postholes, mixed and poured cement, assembled the sections of pen walls, and attached the gate. Since the complicated part of the project had been prefabricated during the week, our work went very fast. Two hours after we had begun, we were sitting on the ground admiring our handiwork.

"It's a great bison pen," said Coleman.

"It's too small," said Brenda.

"It's bigger than the garage."

"Not by much." Brenda was starting to sulk. "She's a wild animal. She needs space. Room to move. Freedom."

"What's the matter with you, Brenda? Flo's got the entire field to roam in when she's not locked up. This is just like a stall in a barn," said Slick, "and our chubby wild bison is getting tamer by the minute."

"She's hungry," I announced.

"Who? Flo?" asked Coleman.

"No, Brenda. She gets irritable in the morning if she hasn't eaten. You didn't eat breakfast, did you, Brenda?" I put my arm around my friend's shoulder.

"No. I'm starving. What time is it, anyway?"

"Twenty minutes to nine," said Coleman. "Where can we get breakfast?"

"Don't look at me. Donuts from the Sea does not serve breakfast," said Augie.

"The diner," announced Slick.

"I don't have any money with me," said Brenda.

"My treat," said Slick, and then saw our eager expressions. "For Brenda, not for the rest of you."

"I wonder if that counts as a date?" I asked.

170

"Did going to the movies with me count as a date?" Coleman smiled at me.

"I'm still deciding." I smiled back at him. The Boys made rude noises. We piled in the truck and went to breakfast.

At exactly eleven o'clock, Augie backed up his truck to Flo's garage stall. We opened the stall gate and slid a wooden ramp into place. Flo looked at us suspiciously. Brenda held out a cookie. Flo took a step forward.

"Progress," I said.

"Look how much fatter she is than last week," said Coleman.

"Who? Brenda?" I asked innocently.

Brenda took a swing at me before feeding Flo another cookie.

"Bison always put on fat in the summer and use it up in the winter. All grazing and browsing animals do that so they are able to survive during the cold season when grass and other foods are scarce. As cold saps their bodily resources, the fat layer provides energy and helps keep them warm," said Coleman, the animal-expert-at-large.

"In that case, Flo looks like she'll be real cozy until next spring."

Flo had reached the bottom of the ramp, where she seemed to have become rooted to the ground. Nothing Brenda did would get her to move a foot.

"Stalemate."

"What are we going to do? We can't lift her."

"Maybe we can walk her to school."

"Sure, right through Florence in broad daylight."

"We can wait until night."

"And what happens if a dog decides to chase her or a car scares her? Buffalo stampede, that's what." We were getting worried. It was now noon, and Flo had moved approximately five feet in an hour.

"Have patience." Brenda walked up the ramp into the truck. She held the bag of cookies in the air and then deliberately emptied it onto the truck floor. Flo watched her and grunted. Brenda cooed to Flo. Flo snorted and sniffed the air. Brenda picked up a cookie from the pile on the floor and took a bite out of it. Flo pawed the ground and grunted again. Brenda chewed and said, "Ummmmm. Goooood."

"Brenda Tuna, get out of there this minute." Ms. Samansky had been inside her house on the telephone. "You will be hurt if Flo panics."

As she spoke, Florence Buffalo made her decision. She charged up the ramp as quickly as possible and skidded to a stop in front of the cookies. Brenda flattened herself against the truck wall. Once Flo was eating, Brenda eased herself around the bison and down the ramp. We shut the back doors and Augie got into the cab. He started the motor and waited. There was no noise from Flo.

"I should ride with her," said Brenda.

"You will ride with Augustus in the cab," ordered Ms. Samansky. "We will meet you at the field."

Ms. Samansky drove like a maniac. We took a shortcut to school, which involved driving through at least one empty lot at the end of a dead-end street. We arrived at school quite a few minutes before the truck.

Brenda insisted that Flo be let out onto the field.

"That might be tricky," said Augie. "Are you sure you don't want to try to get her into her pen now?"

"No, we decided. Flo has to get used to the field. Besides, she needs the exercise. We'll round her up tomorrow morning before school."

172

"Sure you will," said Augie. "Are all the gates closed?"

"And padlocked," said Slick. "Nobody can get in here without our permission."

"I was thinking more about Flo getting out," said Augie.

We put the ramp in place, opened the truck doors, and stepped back. Flo looked up. She finished chewing the last cookie, walked to the opening, saw the possibility of freedom, and practically flew out of the truck. She charged across the field, made a sharp turn at the bleachers, and headed for the fence.

"Uh-oh," I said as Flo hit the chain-link with a mighty crash, bounced off, and shook her head a few times.

"She's hurt," moaned Brenda as she started toward Flo.

"Hold on to that girl," ordered Ms. Samansky. "Flo seems to be a little out of control right now."

Flo put her head down, pawed the ground with her feet, and then ran at the fence once more.

"How is the fence holding up?" asked Charles.

"How can you think of the fence at a time like this?" wailed Brenda. We were holding her arms to keep her away from Flo.

"It's a little bent but I think it's winning the battle."

Flo seemed to think so, too. She walked up to the fence, sniffed it, pushed at it with her head a few times, and then turned her back on it. It was at that moment that Flo finally noticed the grass. She lowered her head and started to eat. And eat. We watched for a full half hour as she slowly made her way across the football field.

"She hasn't come up for air once," said Charles.

"Bison breath through their nostrils. They eat with their mouths," said Coleman. "They do not have to 'come up for air'!"

"It's just an expression."

"I've got to go. Sunday rush at the restaurant. You coming, Cookie?" said Augie.

"Good luck," said Ms. Samansky. "Tomorrow should be a very interesting day."

"You're leaving?" I felt a moment of panic.

"It is, after all, your project. However, I will be available when the trouble begins." Ms. Samansky and Augie drove to the gate, which was opened by The Boys.

"Now what?" asked Coleman.

"We bison-sit," I said.

"For how long?" he asked.

"India and I are staying all night." Brenda was returning from the field house. "Do you think you can get into the field house so we can get water for the bison and use the pay phone?"

"No sweat," said Coleman. "Lock-picking is a lifetime skill, like chili-eating."

"What do you mean, 'staying all night.' Where will we sleep? What if Flo decides to trample us in the night?"

"More likely she'll want to cuddle, but if you're nervous, we can set up the tent inside the pen."

"What tent?"

"My tent—from home."

"How is it going to get here, walk?"

"My mother is bringing it—along with ice, food, and a couple of batches of cookies for Flo."

"Did you communicate telepathically?" asked Slick.

"I communicated with her last night when I was at home."

"You told her about Florence Buffalo?"

"And she didn't ground you?"

"Was she angry?"

"What about *my* parents?" I asked.

"Yes, no, no, and she'll handle them," said Brenda as a horn honked at a side gate to the field.

Brenda's mother delivered two tents, one hibachi, a camp stove, two lanterns, an ice chest full of perishable food, soda, pots and pans, a box of miscellaneous dried foods, seven sleeping bags, an armload of Booster costumes, and a chilling message.

"Greetings from your parents," she said.

"Whose parents?"

"Those parents belonging to you, the Booster Executive Committee."

"You told our parents about the bison? How could you, Mrs. Tuna?"

"I'm a goner."

"I'll be locked in my room for a year."

"Betrayed."

"Sunk."

"I might as well join the foreign legion."

"Nonsense. The news of the bison is old news. We've known about your plans for at least two weeks." Mrs. Tuna was sorting the pile of Booster outfits.

"My father, the conservative engineer, has known about this and hasn't done anything to me?" Charles looked stunned.

"Why don't you ask your father about some of the pranks he participated in when he was in college?" suggested Mrs. Tuna.

"I didn't even know you knew my father," said Charles.

"The parents of the Booster Executive Committee have been meeting weekly almost since you decided to form the Buffalo Boosters."

"They have?"

"We have."

"Why?"

"To exchange information, of course. We love and care about you. We also trust you—completely—except in matters that involve your joint group activities and school."

"Where did this information you exchanged come from?" asked Brenda.

"Mostly from me. You did choose to have the majority of your meetings at our house, you know. . . ."

"You spied on us!" accused Slick.

"Certainly. I eavesdropped."

"You ratted on us!" accused a Boy.

"Certainly."

"Does Ms. Samansky know that you know?"

"I informed her on Tuesday. She was relieved."

"Did you know the bison had arrived before Brenda told you last night?"

"Didn't you think I would be suspicious about being asked to bake three hundred and fifty Rumanian oatmeal-raisin cookies in one week? Besides, Grandpa Tuna spilled the beans."

"*No!*" Brenda was shocked.

"He's very proud of you—all of you. He thinks you're helping to save a piece of the American past. As for the Booster parents, we are uncertain of what the outcome of this project will be, but we have decided to support you."

"Why?"

"Each parent has his or her own reasons. You may call home and get that answer personally. Here's change for the phone." Mrs. Tuna handed us several dollars' worth of change, hugged Brenda, and started to leave.

"Oh, one more thing. All of you are to stay here tonight."

"See, we've been banished."

"Kicked out."

"Rejected."

"Don't be idiots. You are staying to protect Brenda and

176

India. Boys, use the large tent. Brenda will show you how to assemble it. Try not to get expelled tomorrow." Mrs. Tuna left.

The rest of the day felt like a camping trip in the old west. We cooked food over an open fire, watched the bison graze, and discussed the strangeness of parents. Just before dusk, we tacked an enormous banner we had made during the week to the roof of the field house facing the school. THE BUFFALO BOOSTERS WELCOME FLORENCE BUFFALO!

We each telephoned home, and Brenda called the chairpersons of the Booster committees to give them instructions.

"Let's set up the tents now. It's dark enough so no one will notice them," I suggested.

With Brenda shouting directions and a whole lot of swearing and complaining coming from the male committee members, the tents were up in less than half an hour.

"That should have taken only ten minutes."

"Don't be smug, Brenda."

"Okay. Anyone want toasted marshmallows?"

At about nine-thirty, we were exhausted. We had turned off the lanterns and were sitting looking at the stars.

"What a day."

"Tomorrow is going to be something."

"Yeah, something else."

"Do you think they'll expel us?"

"Maybe."

"No."

"Why not?"

"I don't know."

"I'm tired."

"Me, too."

"Let's turn in."

"Good idea."

Just as I was drifting off to sleep, Brenda said, in a very loud voice, "My mother did an underhanded, adult thing. She spied on me. Isn't that great!"

"You're nuts," shouted a Boy from the other tent.

The last thing I heard that night was Flo blowing bubbles in the water tub, which we had left just outside the pen.

▽ ▽ ▽

TWENTY-SIX

"CATCHY tune." Coleman crawled out of the big tent.

Brenda had awakened us by singing reveille at the top of her lungs.

"A bugle would have been less grating." Charles moaned as he struggled to get his arm into his vest.

"So this is the crack of dawn. Interesting." Slick was wearing the full Booster outfit.

"Is that a sunrise?" yawned a Boy.

"No, that's still the moon, idiot," said the other Boy.

"Where's Flo?" I asked.

Brenda pointed to the end of the field and continued stirring something in a large pot.

"Is that food?" Coleman looked alert.

"Oatmeal. It's almost ready," said Brenda.

"Who cares?"

"I want bacon and eggs."

"I don't eat white mushy stuff."

"Oatmeal is white lumpy stuff."

"I don't eat that, either."

"So make yourself some toast. Here's a fork and the bread." Brenda was annoyed.

"How? Where's the toaster?"

"We're in the middle of a field, idiot. Use the flame from the other camp stove." Brenda began dishing stiff globs of oatmeal onto plates.

"Do you know that it's only five-fifteen?" said Slick, gamely mixing butter, milk, and honey into his cereal.

"Of course I do. We have to round up Flo and decide exactly what to do next."

"Besides go to jail?"

"We're not going to go to jail."

"Tell that to Bingham."

"You are very unpleasant in the morning, India," said Brenda.

"Eat oatmeal!" I said as I buttered a piece of burned toast. "Didn't your mother pack any eggs?"

"Of course she did. Oatmeal is better for you."

Coleman and I dove for the cooler and in ten minutes were serving everyone perfectly cooked scrambled eggs.

"Now I can function," said a Boy.

"Good, because we have to get these tents down so we can move Flo into the pen," said Brenda, looking at her watch. "It's already five-forty-five."

"Horrors! The day has just flown past."

At six o'clock, Brenda set across the field toward Florence Buffalo. "I hope Flo recognizes her," said Slick.

"She'll recognize the cookies. Who's coming?" Cars were arriving on the street nearest the football field.

"From the clothing, I'd say Boosters," said Coleman. "One of us had better go over and tell them to keep quiet so they don't spook Flo."

I ran over to the main gate and explained the situation to the Boosters. As I spoke, more arrived.

"This is great," someone whispered.

"A real buffalo."

"Can we pet it?"

"It's wild," I said, "but we're taming it. You're not angry that we spent a bunch of Booster money to bring her here?"

"Are you kidding? We'll go down in Florence High School history. Look how she's following Brenda—just like a big dog."

"Yeah. Buffalo Brenda—just like Buffalo Bill."

"Buffalo Bill killed bison by the thousands," I reminded the speaker.

"This is better," said the kid.

"It sure is. Buffalo Brenda."

"The bison's name is Florence. We call her Flo." I was trying to change the direction of their thoughts.

"Hey, that's neat. Florence Buffalo and Buffalo Brenda." The two names rippled through the growing crowd. I returned to my friends.

"Buffalo Brenda," I said to the Booster Executives as they readied the pen for Flo.

"What?" asked Slick.

"That's what they're calling her, Buffalo Brenda."

"I think I'm jealous," said Coleman.

"Buffalo Coleman wouldn't sound right," said Charles.

"She's going to hate it," I said.

"No way," said Coleman.

"Hate what?" asked Brenda as she led Flo into the pen. Flo sniffed at the pile of hay and took a drink from her tub.

"Nothing," I said.

"Buffalo Brenda," said Coleman.

180

"WHAT?" screamed Brenda. Flo backed into a corner.

"The Boosters have given you a nickname," I said. "They couldn't be dissuaded."

"I hate it," said Brenda, offering Flo another cookie.

"I think you may be stuck with it," I said.

"I guess I've been called worse."

"Definitely."

"Here comes trouble," announced Slick.

The football team had arrived at the field for their preschool morning run. The coach was yanking at the gate, which was chained and locked.

"I'd better let them in," said Slick.

Before going to sleep, we had had a serious debate about whether we should let the teams and gym classes use the athletic field. The Boys favored barricading ourselves on the field until the school officially accepted Florence Buffalo. The rest of us thought it was good politics to allow normal use of the field to prove that Flo was no problem. We won the vote.

"Oh, no, STOP THEM!" I shouted as the football players, without apparently noticing us, began their run around the track.

"Why?" asked Coleman.

"Buffalo chips! We haven't cleaned the field. Stop them. Uh-oh, too late."

Unfortunately it was the coach, running backward on the grassy field, who stepped into a pile of fairly fresh bison dung. Actually, he sort of skidded before sitting hard on the ground. When he realized what had happened, it was as though he suddenly woke up. He noticed us, our folded tents, our camping gear, the pen, and Flo. He blew a steady, ear-shattering blast on his whistle and headed toward us.

"Stop that!" ordered Brenda as the coach got nearer. Flo began pacing back and forth and shaking her head. "STOP!"

181

shouted Brenda. She flung herself in front of the coach and pulled the whistle out of his mouth. He had no choice. He stopped.

Their conversation was very brief. He ordered the team to "stay put" and headed for the school. The football team wandered over to the pen. The players loved Flo. Brenda handed the captain a cookie and after a few minutes, Flo took it from his hand. Slick unlocked the main gates and let the Boosters onto the field. The area around the bison pen was a solid mass of students. For a full fifteen minutes all you could hear were sighs and coos and quiet words of admiration from the crowd. Flo munched hay and appeared to soak up the good feelings. She was absolutely calm.

"What are you going to do with her?" someone finally asked.

"We," said Brenda. "What are *we* going to do with her. Florence Buffalo is the new mascot of Florence Senior High School. She belongs to each and every one of you. She will bring us good luck. Her bison fortitude and courage will lead us to victory. Flo is a symbol of our strength. She is a symbol of America. . . ."

"Enough," I whispered to Brenda. "Don't lay it on too thick."

"I was on a roll," said Brenda.

"You are on your way out of this school," boomed a dreaded voice. The awful Osgood was shoving students aside and pushing his way toward us. The coach was behind him.

"What are you doing here?" I asked.

"I don't have to ask the same question of you, do I, Miss Delinquent!"

"Ms. Delinquent," I said before I could stop myself.

"Delinquent is the key word, Inkblot. Mr. Bingham and his staff are at a regional meeting this morning. I am in charge of the school until he returns. You are under my jurisdiction. I expel you—all of you." Mr. Osgood gestured to the crowd, which included the entire football team. The coach grabbed his arm and whispered in Osgood's ear.

"Except the football team," amended Osgood.

"You'll have to expel all of us," said a voice.

"Who spoke?" asked the astonished coach.

"Me, Peter," said the captain of the team. "Flo is our bison, too."

"Yeah," agreed the team. "Our bison."

"Go take showers!" ordered the coach.

The football team ignored him.

"Please. Don't get yourselves expelled over something you're not responsible for," pleaded Brenda. "They're all innocent, Osgood, including the Boosters. Let them go."

"No, we're not, Buffalo Brenda. The Executives acted in our name and we're proud of what you did. We're as guilty as you are! *Semper Fidelis*, Forever Faithful," shouted a Booster.

"That's the motto of the Marine Corps," complained Osgood.

"If it's good enough for them, it's good enough for us," said the Booster.

"You might as well conserve your energies for something worthwhile—like saving your own necks. Before coming down to this field, I contacted Arnic's Abattoir. A truck will be here at noon to pick up your bison. By afternoon, there will be no trace of the bison or the Booster Executive Committee on school property."

"What's an abattoir?" asked a Booster.

"A fancy name for a slaughterhouse. He's planning to make meat out of Florence Buffalo," said Brenda, "and we won't let him."

183

"Try and stop me," said Osgood. "This is school property and I am in charge."

"You're nuts," said Slick.

"Completely," said a Boy.

"Follow me," said Osgood, turning toward the gate. "The so-called Booster Executives will spend the morning in the detention room. The rest of you misguided lemmings will go to your classes. Your fate will be sealed when Mr. Bingham returns."

Everyone looked at Brenda. She nodded and began following Osgood and the coach toward the gate. Brenda walked slower and slower. We took baby steps behind her. As the coach and Osgood passed through the gate, Brenda rushed forward and slammed it. The football team threw their bodies against it. The Boys wrapped the chain around the upright posts, and Coleman clamped a lock onto it. Osgood, hearing the gate clank shut, turned and glared at us.

"Men, please," pleaded the coach.

"Nobody's going to chop up our mascot," growled a very angry fullback.

"Nobody," we all agreed.

Osgood and the coach stomped up the hill toward the school.

"Now what?" someone asked.

"I'm not sure, but something will occur to me," said Brenda.

"It had better," I said. "Look at Flo, I think she's sick."

Florence Buffalo was standing in the middle of her pen. Her mouth was open, she was breathing very hard, her head was bobbing up and down with each breath.

"Maybe she's just excited," said a Boy.

Flo made a loud and terrible sound and sank to her knees.

"She's in pain." Brenda raced to the pen. We all followed. "What's wrong?"

"Maybe Osgood poisoned her."

"Maybe someone shot her."

"Call a vet."

My hands were shaking as I flipped through the pages of the phone book.

"Please, God, don't let Florence Buffalo die," I whispered.

"Amen," whispered Coleman, who was dropping coins into the pay phone.

▽ ▽ ▽

TWENTY-SEVEN

BRENDA was sitting on the ground in the bison pen, cradling Flo's enormous head in her lap. An uneaten Rumanian oatmeal-raisin cookie lay on the ground in front of Flo's nose.

"The veterinarian is on his way, Brenda. He'll be here in fifteen minutes."

Brenda nodded and whispered something to Flo.

"I'll stand by the gate to let him in," said Slick.

"We'll go with you just in case," said Peter.

"Just in case what?" asked Charles.

"Just in case anyone tries to bully his way in with the vet."

"Good idea."

Flo was panting rapidly. Her eyes were glazed. I was really scared, but I couldn't let Brenda know.

"She's going to be fine, Bren." I hugged Brenda, who had started to cry.

There was shouting on the hill near the school. A great many students were trying to come down the hill to the football field. Teachers and custodians were blocking the paths. Other students were hanging out classroom windows, trying to catch a glimpse of Flo.

"I hope they get to see more than a buffalo hide," mumbled Coleman. Gasps of horror came from the Boosters standing near him.

He was saved from a possible pummeling by the action on the hilltop. A small person with a pack on her back broke through the cordon of teachers and custodians and raced toward the field.

"It couldn't be," said a Boy.

"It sure is. LET HER IN!" the other Boy shouted to Slick, who rapidly unwound the chain from the gate.

"I didn't think an old person could run that fast."

"Maybe she works out."

"Osgood is going to catch her."

"No way."

Ms. Samansky slid through the open gate a split second before the Florence Buffalo tackles slammed it in Osgood's face.

"You're fired, Samansky!" Osgood shouted at her back.

"Hah!" said Ms. Samansky.

"I hope he has chain-link marks on his face for the rest of his life," said a Booster.

Ms. Samansky arrived at the bison pen out of breath and smiling—until she saw Flo. She knelt down next to the bison and ran her hands over Flo's stomach.

"A vet is on the way, Ms. Samansky," I said.

Ms. Samansky appeared not to hear me. She continued her examination of Flo. She lifted Flo's tail, nodded her head, and began to give us orders.

"Buckets of hot water, soap, towels, lots of fresh hay—spread it around Florence—a pair of scissors, some string—and be quick about it—there's not much time."

"Oh, no, she's going to die," wailed Brenda, flinging herself over Flo's heaving body.

"Brenda Tuna, get off the bison and let her have her contractions in peace. And why aren't the rest of you getting what I asked for? This bison is going to have a calf. A sterile environment would be helpful." Ms. Samansky glowered at the crowd of frozen Boosters. "MOVE!"

"A calf?"

"A bison baby?"

"It's the wrong time of year," said Coleman.

"Who cares?"

"In the wild, a bison born in the fall would probably not make it through winter," Coleman explained.

"This isn't the wild, it's the suburbs."

"Yes, but . . ." began Coleman.

"Shut up, Coleman. All that matters is that Flo's having a baby," said Brenda.

"FLO'S HAVING A BISON BABY!" The Boosters were shouting and jumping up and down.

"Someone go tell Slick and the team. And all screamers and jumpers either quiet down or go over to the bleachers. You're bothering Flo." I found myself giving orders to people.

"I think they heard the shouting. From the looks of it, everyone at school has." In fact, the kids on the hill and in the building were going crazy.

By the time the vet arrived, there wasn't much left for him to do but wait.

"Ever delivered something this big?" he asked Ms. Samansky, who nodded.

"A horse?" he asked.

"A giraffe," she said. When we all stared at her, Ms. Samansky said, "It's a long story. Now's not the time."

"Yes, it is," said the vet, and moved behind Flo.

At that moment a truck pulled up to the gate. A roar of anger came from the students.

"Arnie's Abattoir has arrived," said Coleman.

"So has Bingham. Look!" said Charles.

"And who are they?" asked a Booster.

The field parking lot was filling up with cars full of adults.

"Citizens of Florence," I said. "Any of you Boosters call home?" A few hands tentatively went up. "Don't be ashamed. The rest of you call home, now. The more people we have as witnesses, the less chance there is they'll hurt Flo."

Bingham was carrying his bullhorn. "TIME IS UP! Those of you responsible for this, come forward IMMEDIATELY!" Naturally we ignored him. The baby bison had begun to enter the world.

"I think I'm going to faint," said Charles.

"Me, too," said a Booster.

"OPEN THIS GATE. YOU ARE TRESPASSING!" squawked Bingham.

"Fainters go to the gate and help the team. Tell Bingham what's happening and tell him to shut up. He's making Flo nervous. Look, some custodians are trying to cut the chains on the side gate. Warn the football team!" I gave the orders almost without thinking. I wasn't surprised that people did as I said.

"Has Brenda been practicing ventriloquism or was that really you, India?" asked a Boy.

"Its legs are coming out," said a Booster.

Flo grunted, gave one last mighty push, and the baby bison was lying on the clean hay. A sigh went through the crowd as Flo began licking her calf. Brenda was smiling so hard I thought her face would break. It was time for me to do what I had to do.

"Where are you going, India?" asked Brenda.

"Every army needs a general," I said.

"And every general must have a plan to maintain the confidence of her troops," advised my friend.

"I don't have a plan," I said.

"Then do what all good generals do—invent one on the spot."

It was good advice so I took it. By the time I reached the main gate, I knew what I had to do and how I was going to do it.

"Where is Tunafish?" demanded Osgood, who was standing next to Bingham.

"Shut up, Osgood," said Mr. Bingham. "Miss Teidlebaum, where is Miss Tuna?

"Brenda is helping Florence Buffalo, Mr. Bingham."

"Two cows for the meat market," smirked Osgood.

"What are you talking about?" asked Mr. Bingham.

"He's trying to send our bison to Arnie's Abattoir," I said in quite a loud voice.

"The slaughterhouse?" said a shocked adult bystander. "The school is planning to send those beautiful creatures to the slaughterhouse?"

"No, we are not," insisted Mr. Bingham.

As he spoke, the students on the hill broke through the human cordon and rushed toward the field.

"Oh, no," groaned Bingham.

About thirty students swarmed onto the truck, making it impossible for it to be driven.

"What kind of irresponsible decisions are being made here?" asked a well-dressed man. "This is a harmless prank and you intend to end it by killing a rare animal—a national symbol? I am a lawyer and will be happy to represent these students and their bison." He passed his card to me through the fence.

"Nobody needs a lawyer. *No* decision has been made—yet. But nobody is going to kill these animals. Osgood, send the truck away," ordered Bingham.

"Then we can keep Florence Buffalo and her baby, Mr. Bingham," I said.

"No."

"But they're the school mascots."

"They're to be gone from here tonight. If you don't let us in, we'll cut our way through the fence and bill your parents for the damage."

"You'll have to go over my body to get to the bison," I said, and lay down on the ground.

"Right!" said Slick, and lay down next to me.

"Double right!" said Peter.

In a minute all the Boosters, the football team, and several hundred students outside the fence were lying on the ground.

"You have disrupted the entire school day," shouted Bingham.

I leaned on my elbow. "It's not *our* school day. Osgood expelled all of us."

"I rescind the expulsion." Everyone whistled and applauded, including the adults. "Now will you get back to school?"

"What about Flo and Tuna Surprise?" asked a Booster.

"Who?" I asked.

"That's what we decided to call the baby. It fits."

"It fits perfectly. Does Brenda know?"

"No."

"Good."

"They go," said Mr. Bingham.

"Where?"

"Where they came from—anywhere—to a zoo, to a farm—to the pound."

"I don't pick up nothing bigger than a dog." The town animal warden had pushed his way through the crowd.

"Go away," said Mr. Bingham. The animal warden said a few rude words and left.

"The bison have to stay until tomorrow night," I said.

"What happens tomorrow?"

"The Glen Harbor Devils are coming her at four o'clock to play a football game."

Mr. Bingham turned pale. The students were suddenly silent. "On a Tuesday?"

"The scheduled game was rained out."

Mr. Bingham turned to the coach. "Couldn't it have been canceled entirely? Where was your head?"

"I tried, but they insisted we play them. They said something about tradition." The coach stared at the ground as he spoke.

"Why do the bison have to be here?" asked Bingham.

"Because if they're here, the Buffalos will win," I said, and waited for the reaction.

The entire crowd of protesters sat up. Mouths fell open. People were looking at me in disbelief.

"You're as bad as your buddy," whispered Slick.

"Thank you," I said quietly, and stood up.

"Friends, teachers, parents, and other miscellaneous adults," I began, "as you know, the Glen Harbor Devils have beaten the Florence Buffalos every year for twenty-two years. More accurately, they have mercilessly inflicted pain and humiliation on our team—taking delight in causing as many bruises and sprains as possible during each play. For twenty-one years, nobody at Florence High has looked forward to the annual game.

191

Attendance by Florence fans at the painful games has dropped to near invisible levels—leaving our noble team of brave men to face the barbarians alone."

"Get to the point, India, before you lose them," Slick warned, but I could see the faces in the crowd—they were hanging on my every word.

"This year will be different. Florence Buffalo and Tuna Surprise have changed our luck."

"They have?" asked a team member.

"You bet. Tomorrow every student, every teacher, every citizen *must* be here to cheer for the Florence Buffalos. Glen Harbor will try to give us its worst, but we will stand against them with our *best*—AND WE WILL WIN!"

The students screamed, the adults applauded, the players pounded each other on the back, and Bingham shoved his arm between the gate and the fence and grabbed me behind the neck.

"You have until tomorrow night, young woman, and then the bison are a thing of the past."

"You may change your mind, sir," I said.

"And the moon is made of green cheese," said Bingham.

"For an educator, that's very inflexible thinking." Ms. Samansky had joined us.

"You're fired, Samansky," said Bingham.

"Too late. My letter of resignation has been in your mailbox since early morning. Come, India, we have work to do."

"One more thing," Bingham called after us. "The Buffalos had better win tomorrow."

"There's no way they can lose," I said.

"When did you fix the game?" asked Slick, catching up to us.

"How did you do it—bribery, threats, extortion?" said a Boy.

"I was just being mathematically accurate," I said.

"How?"

"There's no *one* way the Buffalos can lose the game—there are probably a hundred ways."

"A thousand ways."

"A million ways."

"*No* way." Brenda was back among the human beings. "We're going to win. I have a plan."

"I'm the general here. You're the buffalo-keeper," I complained.

"The plan involves buffalo."

"Naturally."

▽ ▽ ▽

TWENTY-EIGHT

THE Booster Executive Parents showed up at the field at around three in the afternoon. They brought us food supplies, clothing, a message, and a warning. The message was that they loved us and wished us well. The warning was that we had better not get ourselves expelled.

"I don't care, I'm not going to school tomorrow," said Brenda. "What are my parents going to do, cast me out if I get expelled?"

"It's a possibility," I said. "Why don't we divide the day into sections—we can take shifts staying here with the bison and also go to some classes."

"I'm staying all day," insisted Brenda.

"Me, too," said Slick.

In the end, we decided to stick together. At around five, the members of the football team, having practiced all afternoon, were lying on the grass exhausted.

"We're going to get killed."

"Creamed."

"Mangled."

"Destroyed."

"No way," said Brenda. "Follow me."

They dragged themselves to their feet and shuffled over to the bison pen. Brenda opened the gate. Flo stepped between Tuna Surprise and the invaders. She lowered her head.

"Uh-oh," said Coleman.

Brenda handed me a large bag of cookies and walked over to Flo. She draped an arm around Flo's neck and gestured to the team with the other.

"Give them each a piece of cookie, India. One at a time, men," she ordered.

Peter went first. He walked toward Flo with the cookie in his hand. Flo sniffed at it and then sucked it into her mouth.

"Put your hand on her head, Peter, and feel her great strength," said Brenda.

Peter lay his hand on Flo's huge cranium. He left it there for a minute. Soon he was smiling. He looked peaceful. He began to look confident. He turned to his teammates. "We're going to win," he said.

That evening we arranged our tents around the outside of the bison pen. To make guarding them easier, we had decided to keep Flo and Tuna Surprise confined. Ms. Samansky had remained with us, but she hadn't said much since she'd told Bingham she had quit her job.

"Is Augie coming here tonight, Ms. Samansky?" I asked.

"He's making important arrangements," she said, "regarding our future." Ms. Samansky proceeded to empty the pack she had been wearing earlier in the day. She unrolled a small tent, a sleeping bag, a foam mattress, and a long, thick chain. "As for me, I'm staying to the bitter end."

"Why do you have a chain in your pack?" asked a Boy.

"As a last resort."

"I don't understand."

"I do," said Brenda. "Ms. Samansky is prepared to chain herself in protest to whatever is appropriate."

"That's crazy," said Charles.

"Your imagination is limited," said Ms. Samansky. "Tomorrow is going to be a trying day. We may be called upon to make use of unusual and extreme measures."

"What's going to happen to Flo and Tuna Surprise?" asked a Boy.

"Please call her something else," said Brenda.

"But Tuna Surprise is her name."

"I hate it."

"Who cares?"

"After we win the game, they're going to let us keep the bison," said Brenda.

"Now that's imagination."

"And if we lose?"

"We can't lose."

"The team is gone for the night, so we can be honest with ourselves. We can't win."

Nobody slept much that night. The early part of Tuesday was uneventful, which gave us plenty of time to worry. Just after three o'clock Florence fans began sneaking into their own stadium. By three-forty-five every available seat in the home-team section was occupied by a silent, nervous person. The Glen

Harbor students seemed to arrive as a unit. At three-forty-five their seats were empty, and at three-fifty the visitors' bleachers were completely filled with hooting, jeering maniacs.

Brenda stayed in the pen with Flo and Tuna Surprise, keeping Flo calm with a steady supply of cookies. At exactly four o'clock the Glen Harbor Devils rushed onto the field, looking mean and bloodthirsty. The Buffalos began the traditional run, when suddenly, they made a sharp, unexpected, left turn and headed for the bison pen. They repeated the bison petting and feeding ritual of the day before, only this time, after each team member touched Flo, Brenda handed him a small piece of bison fur that he tucked into his shoe. The whole effect was magical. Even the Devil fans were silent.

At halftime nobody had scored and not a single Florence player had been injured. The Devil fans were amazed and angry. The Buffalo fans were dazed and joyful. During halftime the Buffalos again visited Flo. Brenda went into a huddle with the team. Before anyone could stop them, Brenda led Flo out of the pen and a player closed the gate on Tuna Surprise, locking her in. The team formed a protective circle around Flo as Brenda led her to the middle of the fifty-yard line where the Devils were angrily waiting for the kickoff.

Just as the strange procession reached the exact center of the field, the Florence Buffalos broke the circle and took their playing positions behind Flo. Brenda stopped shoving cookies into Flo's mouth. This caused Flo to look away from Brenda's hand. She looked behind herself. She looked to both sides. She glanced at the Devils, whom she happened to be facing. She did not see what she wanted to see. Flo raised her head and bellowed. Tuna Surprise, never having been more than a few feet from her mother and now locked in her pen, answered Flo with loud, frantic cries.

To understand what happened next, you have to know two things. First, facing a bison close up under the best of circumstances is an awesome experience. Second, the bison pen was in a corner of the field behind the Glen Harbor Devils.

When Flo put her head down and began her charge, it looked to the Devils as if she had gone mad and was about to squash them into a collective pulp. They scattered, screaming in terror. Flo galloped directly to the pen, where I was standing holding the gate open. In less than thirty seconds from the time Flo had noticed her absence, Tuna Surprise was nursing happily and loudly and Flo was munching on hay. She wasn't even breathing hard.

During all of this commotion, the Florence Buffalos stood quietly, hands on hips, looking strong and confident. They won the game—or, as some might insist, the demoralized Devils lost the game. The melee that followed wasn't pretty. The Glen Harbor fans, assuming that they had been tricked, tore up the stands, the goalposts, the grass on the field, and tried to pick fights with whatever Florence fans were dumb enough to stick around.

The Booster Executives, aided by a few reckless Boosters and members of the football team, surrounded the bison pen. It was the sound of sirens that made the advancing mob hesitate long enough for Mr. Bingham and a delegation of adults to reach us.

"Have you made plans for their leave-taking?" Bingham asked, pointing to the bison.

"Didn't you see the game?" asked Brenda.

"I also saw that dangerous stunt you pulled. They go— tonight."

"We haven't exactly made the arrangements," I said. "Couldn't you give us a few more days?"

"You have until midnight tonight. After that, the bison are my responsibility."

"Then what? You sell them for buffalo burgers?"

"Midnight!" said Bingham, and stalked off the field with his entourage.

"Who were those people?"

"I think one of them is on the school board."

"Their leaving is more important than their identity," I said.

"Why?"

"We're being attacked." The brief meeting with Bingham had given the Devil fanatics a chance to catch their breath and organize. While most of them were being herded off the field to their cars and buses, a determined group of about forty had broken away and were now heading toward us.

"They look a little angry," said a Booster whose voice was shaking.

"This is it, the end—all my plans down the toilet—what irony—a football game—I don't even like football. . . ." Charles was mumbling to himself.

"We can run. They haven't surrounded us yet."

"And leave the bison after they helped us win the game?" Peter was standing shoulder to shoulder with Slick and The Boys and about half the football team.

The growling mob was about fifty feet from us. Ms. Samansky suddenly stepped in front of our line of defense, swinging her folded chain gently against her legs.

"Back off, bozos," she threatened, "or take the consequences."

The Glen Harbor students stopped—probably more out of shock than fear.

"What do you think you're doing, lady?" shouted a kid.

Before she could answer, a truck roared onto the field blasting its horn. It cut through the end zone and came to a stop between us and our enemies. Augie jumped out of the passenger side of the cab. Grandpa Tuna blew the horn once more, turned off the engine, and swung his legs out of the cab on the driver's side. Sitting there, towering over the Devils, he straightened his suit jacket and adjusted the peaked cap on his head before starting to speak.

"Go homes, childrens," he said, "before yous bites more den yous can eats."

"Chew, Grandpa," corrected Brenda.

"Shuts up, Grendchild. Lets your grendpa voirk. You hoird me, roughnecks, go home."

"Says who, old man?" shouted a rude Devil fan.

"Says me, kiddo. Don't esk vat it is I hev in da truck. Buts if I lets it out, a sorry bunch of hoodlems you vill be. Gets it?"

"He's bluffing," said a not-so-confident voice.

"What if he has another one of those buffalo things in there? It can mash us, man."

The Glen Harbor vandals were still debating when the police finally worked their way to our end of the field and encouraged them to head toward home.

"Poifect," said Grandpa Tuna. "Now lets gets dis show on da road."

"What show, Grandpa?" asked Brenda.

"Da beginnings of mine future life—George Vashington Tuna of da Nort Voods. Pioneer. Frontneersman. Lumbnerjack. Forest Rangner . . . "

"Grandpa, you live in the Bronx."

"Used to, sveethearts. Betsy Ross, your grendmother, and I are moving to Maine."

"Alone? You'll die. You'll starve to death. You'll be lonely. Why are you doing this?"

As Brenda spoke, Augie was backing the truck up to the bison pen.

"Nots alone. Ve are chartner members of da soon-to-be famnous American Vildlife Rescue Commune and Retirement Refuge and Gourmet Fish Restaurant," said Grandpa Tuna.

"Who's we?" asked Brenda.

"Augala, Cookala, me, and your grendma."

"Augustus and I have owned the land and buildings for a number of years," Ms. Samansky explained. "We've been waiting for the right time to make our move and the right people to move with. Your bison escapade seems to have provided both."

"Why are you doing this, Grandpa?"

"Because ve vants to. Ve are going to be tilling da land, toiling da soil, bakings da breads, takings care of da aneemals— hevings a vonderful time."

"Vladimir . . ." interrupted Ms. Samansky.

"Hokay. Hokay. Cookala is rights. To be absolutny trutful, Grendchild, we hev hired tillers and toilers to do da farm voirk. Ve takings care of da restaurant and da aneemals."

"What animals?" asked Brenda.

"Sick aneemals, hoirt aneemals, aneemals vitouts parents, aneemals vitouts homes—raccoons, bear, deer, bison— vatsever."

"Bison?"

"Ve gots lots of lend, good fencnes, a nice barn . . ."

"You can't just take our bison," said Brenda.

"Brenda, that's your own trusted grandfather, not a bison rustler," I said.

"Trusted? He's deserting me."

"You can visit him."

"You can join their commune."

"No, she can't!" The three adults spoke at once.

"I can't visit you?"

"No, you can'ts *join* us—nots until you are fifty-five years old. Visits venever you likes. Tink about a vacation vere nothing vill eat you, Grendchild." Grandpa Tuna hugged Brenda.

"We'll have to vote, Grandpa. The bison belong to everyone."

Everyone who was present voted to send Florence Buffalo and Tuna Surprise to Maine. Augie and Grandpa Tuna had rented a luxurious transporter. The bison seemed to sense they were in good hands, because they followed Brenda up the ramp and seemed completely at home once in the truck. Tuna Surprise lay down in the straw bedding and Flo munched on some nice, green hay.

In a matter of minutes, the truck was gone. We leaned on the fence and stared at the empty bison pen.

"It happened so fast, I didn't have a chance to really say good-bye." Brenda sobbed.

"Is she talking about her grandfather or the bison?" asked a weeping Booster.

"The bison," I said.

"I was sure Bingham would let us keep our buffalo after today's game," said a player.

"Bison."

"To me they'll always be buffalo."

"I'm going to visit them in Maine."

"They said they'd send pictures and videotapes so we can watch Tuna Surprise grow."

After a while, the Boosters and the team members drifted

away. The Booster Executives had dragged our gear to the parking lot and were waiting for various parents to come get it and us.

"What's next?" asked a Boy.

"How can you even ask that? Let's take a break and recover from this project."

"Why?"

"Because."

"That's no answer."

"We'll never top this in a million years."

"Who says?" Brenda was cheering up.

"Do you have anything in mind?"

"I do," said a Boy.

"Is it interesting?"

"Of course."

"Is it complicated?"

"Is it legal?"

"Does it involve school?"

"It involves all of Florence."

"The whole town?"

"Maybe the county."

"Tell us."

The next night Brenda and I were lying in the sheep meadow looking at the stars.

"They're in Maine. My grandparents called today."

"Are you still sad?" I asked.

"I'm miserable, but it will pass. What do you think of The Boy's idea?"

"I wonder what it's like to be tarred and feathered and run out of town."

"That good, huh? You know life is really what you make it, India Ink."

"I know, Brenda Tuna. Life is just a mixed bowl of fruit. One day it's a banana, one day a peach, and one day a rotten apple. The motto of life should be Squeeze before You Bite," I said, keeping a straight face.

"Amazing I didn't think of that one myself," said Brenda. "Isn't it."